Leave It To Lexie

Leave It
To Lexie

By Lisa Eisenberg

VIKING

For Asafetida

VIKING
Published by the Penguin Group
Viking Penguin, a division of Penguin Books USA Inc.,
40 West 23rd Street, New York, New York 10010, U.S.A.
Penguin Books Ltd, 27 Wrights Lane, London W8 5TZ, England
Penguin Books Australia Ltd, Ringwood, Victoria, Australia
Penguin Books Canada Ltd, 2801 John Street, Markham, Ontario, Canada L3R 1B4
Penguin Books (N.Z.) Ltd, 182–190 Wairau Road, Auckland 10, New Zealand

Penguin Books Ltd, Registered Offices: Harmondsworth, Middlesex, England

First published in 1989 by Viking Penguin, a division of Penguin Books USA Inc.
1 3 5 7 9 10 8 6 4 2
Copyright © Lisa Eisenberg, 1989
All rights reserved

LIBRARY OF CONGRESS CATALOGING-IN-PUBLICATION DATA
Eisenberg, Lisa. Leave it to Lexie
Lisa Eisenberg.   p.   cm.
Summary: Nine-year-old Lexie is at a loss for ideas for the
upcoming Girl Scout talent show, until she remembers her father's
penchant for riddles at dinnertime.
ISBN 0-670-82844-0
[1. Talent shows—Fiction. 2. Girl Scouts—Fiction.] I. Title.
PZ7.E3458Le 1989
[Fic]—dc20   89-9171

Printed in U.S.A.
Set in Times Roman.

Leave It To Lexie

One

Lexie Nielsen flopped backward onto her pillow and used both hands to hoist her right foot up in front of her face.

"You sloppy, scummy, lazy little slob!"

Ignoring the loud, screeching voice, Lexie painstakingly scraped a slimy piece of grass off her long, dirty big toe. When she'd finished with that toe, she moved on to a careful study of the next one and then the next, on down the line. After she'd given her entire foot a microscopic examination, she slowly twisted her head sideways and gazed over at her sister. What she saw didn't surprise her very much. Faith's round face was bright red with anger. Her features were screwed up with rage. Her hands were balled into two white-knuckled fists.

Lexie faked a big, drawn-out yawn. So Faith was ticked off about something, she thought. What else was new? Lately Faith was *always* acting like she was about to short out all her circuits and explode.

"You incredibly unorganized, irresponsible, unsanitary, *grubby*—"

"I get this feeling you're not very happy, Faith," Lexie interrupted. She picked up her other foot and started inspecting her second set of grimy toes. "But that's okay with me. Remember what Mom is always saying about bottling up anger and—"

"Oh, shut up, you little smart aleck! Why do you always have to be such a nasty, mouthy twit?"

Lexie finished with her foot and glanced at the big purple plastic watch she wore strapped around her ankle. Then she rolled off the side of the bed and got up. She was supposed to meet Debby and the other kids at the park in ten minutes, and she'd have to hurry to make it on time. But, as she started toward the door, Faith darted in front of her and blocked her path. "You're not going anywhere, Lexie," she said through clenched teeth. "Not until we finish this conversation."

4

"I'd love to finish this conversation, Faith," Lexie answered. "I'd *kill* to finish this conversation! The only problem is, I don't have the slightest clue what this conversation is about!"

Faith's loud shriek of phony laughter sounded just like Count Dracula's in *Return of the Vengeful Vampire*. "Do you actually mean to say," she said with a flash of her fangs, "that you can stand here in the middle of this putrid pigsty of a room—a room that I am *compelled* against my will to share with you—and claim that you don't know what I'm talking about?"

Lexie yawned for a second time. In her heart, she'd known all along what Faith was mad about, of course. But she could almost never resist the temptation to drive her sister crazy by pretending not to have the slightest idea. Though, come to think of it, that wasn't really all that much fun anymore. These days, it was just too easy to drive Faith right over the brink.

Lexie acted like she'd just noticed something interesting in the corner behind Faith's back. Suddenly, she feinted to the right and then quickly tried to duck back under Faith's outstretched left arm. But her sister was too fast for her. She grabbed Lexie by the shoulders and twisted her around to face back into the room.

"Just look at this dump, this . . . this *sewer system!* How can you live like this, Lexie? More to the point, how can *I* live like this?"

With one more enormous fake yawn, Lexie surveyed the big, sunny, L-shaped bedroom she shared with her older sister. As usual, Faith's half looked as clean and antiseptic as an operating room in a hospital. The floor was absolutely free of clutter, as were the desk and dressing table. The few essential things allowed out of their assigned drawers were lined up in tidy, rigidly organized order, the pencil next to the pen, the text-books next to the notebooks, the brush next to the comb, the lipstick next to the nail polish, etc., etc.

Even Faith's bed looked neat and clean. The sheets, blanket, and bedspread had been stretched to their ab-solute wrinkle-free limit and then firmly wedged in at the edges and secured with four perfect hospital cor-ners. An army drill sergeant could have bounced a penny off the flat, tight surface.

Lexie stared at the bed, and her eyes narrowed. Faith's bed looked different. Somehow it was even neater and cleaner than usual. But how could that be? All at once, Lexie knew how. "Where are all your stuffed animals?" she asked accusingly.

"I put them away in the closet," Faith said shortly. "In a garbage bag."

"Even Bananny?" Lexie gasped in horror. "You stuffed poor old faithful Bananny into a garbage bag in the closet?" Bananny was Faith's favorite battered yel-low teddy bear. She'd been sleeping with it since she was two years old. "Listen, if you don't want him, can I have—"

"We're not here to discuss my childhood toys, Lexie! We're here to discuss what you plan to do about your half of this pigsty."

Reluctantly, Lexie turned her gaze toward her part of the room. As she looked around, she had to confess to herself that things had gotten pretty bad over there. So many stuffed animals, sandals, sneakers, shorts, T-shirts, towels, bathing suits, underpants, board games, decks of cards, schoolbooks, notebooks, and riddle books were piled up on the floor, she could hardly see the bed!

She pulled away from Faith's clutches and shrugged. "It doesn't look that bad to me," she said. "But if it bothers you so much, I'll clean it up when I get back from the park."

She started toward the door again, and again Faith grabbed her shoulders. "You'll clean it up now, you grubby little worm!"

Lexie wrenched herself free and planted her hands on her hips. She'd been putting up with Faith's bossy, insulting ways for a long time now, but this was going too far. "Just stop grabbing me, Faith!" she yelled. "You're not Mom. You can't tell me what to do!"

Faith moved forward and shoved her face right up next to Lexie's. "Speaking of Mom," she said with a sickeningly sweet smile, "don't you think she might be interested in coming in for a look at this room? After all, she's been so busy lately she hasn't had time to check up on things, but if someone were to happen to *invite* her up here, don't you think she just might want to have a little talk with us about our cleaning habits?"

Oh geez, Lexie thought. Faith was really playing dirty now. Their mother was going to graduate school for a master's degree in counseling this year, and she'd become obsessed with having little talks, or what she called "rap sessions," with her children and husband. In her heart of hearts, Lexie knew her mother was having the sessions for a good reason. Mrs. Nielsen always felt terrible when one of her kids was having a problem, and this was just her latest way of trying to help. But even so, Lexie hated the rap sessions with a passion. They were long, boring, embarrassing, and painful. Lexie was secretly convinced that her father hated the sessions just as much as she did, but of course he couldn't say so out loud because adults always have to stick together and present a united front on these things.

Faith knew Lexie would do almost anything to get out of a rap session with their mother. It was a horrible threat to hold over someone's head. If Faith would stoop to that, there was *nothing* she wouldn't do!

My sister has become a complete and total crud,

Lexie said to herself. Out loud, she sighed and said, "All right, all right, all right. You win. I'll clean up." She wandered over toward her half of the room, where she started halfheartedly picking up clothes, books, and toys and stuffing them randomly into her dresser drawers. "It doesn't matter a bit, of course," she said bitterly, "that I already have plans for this afternoon. Or that my friends are all waiting for me. Or that I've had so much on my mind lately."

"Your friends will wait for you as always," Faith said. "They may be babies, but they're loyal." She pulled a Hershey bar out of the pocket of her denim skirt and crossed the room to her dressing table. As she pulled off the shiny brown candy wrapper, she sat down in front of the mirror and started staring at her reflection. "And what on earth could a little fourth-grade twit possibly have on her so-called mind?"

Happy for any excuse to stop cleaning up, Lexie hastily kicked her dirty Disneyland T-shirt under her bed and went over to explain to her sister. "It's the talent show," she said, "for Girl Scouts. For all the parents and grandparents and brothers and sisters and everybody. Two weeks from last Saturday."

"Two weeks from last Saturday," Faith repeated with a frown. She took a big bite of her Hershey bar, and Lexie swallowed a cutting comment. Mom's last rap session with Faith had been about proper eating habits and their beneficial effect on self-esteem. Faith had put on about ten pounds since she'd started seventh grade three weeks ago, and their mother was seriously concerned about it. Chocolate was first on the Forbidden Item list the two of them had drawn up together.

Lexie knew that if she threatened chocolate blackmail she could get at least half of the candy bar for herself, but she decided against it. She was hoping her sister might be able to help her out with the talent show thing, and she didn't want to make her mad again right now.

"Right," she said, plopping herself down on Faith's rigid board of a bed. "The talent show is two weeks from the day before yesterday."

"So what's the big deal about an infantile Girl Scout troop talent show?" Faith asked. She opened the top drawer of the dressing table and pulled out a pair of tiny tweezers.

"The big deal is that I don't want to be in the show. In fact, I'd rather die than be in it!"

"So don't be in it, lamebrain!"

"You're kidding, right, Faith? I mean, do we have the same mother, or what? You know how important she thinks it is for us to be in school activities and stuff. She'll *insist* that I be in the show for my own good!"

Faith grasped the tweezers and leaned forward, closer to the mirror. "If you put up a good enough argument," she said, "Mom would probably let you off the hook.

10

But if you're that worried about it, maybe you just shouldn't tell her about the show."

"Well, I haven't told her about it yet. But Mrs. Noble is writing a notice for us to take home at the next meeting. And you know Mom. She has a way of hearing about these things. It's like she has radar or something."

Faith leaned forward, plucked at an eyebrow hair, and winced. "So why don't you just go ahead and be in the stupid show?" she asked.

"Because I'd rather die, that's why!" Lexie said again. "Because there's nothing in the world I can do! Face it, Faith. I simply do not have any talents!"

Faith zeroed in on another hair. "Don't sell yourself short, Lexie," she said as she tweezed. "You have lots of talents. You have a talent for creating a mess, for not doing your homework, for making me mad, for getting in trouble with Mom and your teachers. . . . I could go on and on."

Lexie felt a surge of hot anger. "You know, you're really a jerk, Faith!" she said. "Here I confide in you about a real problem, and all you can do is be mean, stare at yourself, and tweeze your ugly old eyebrows!"

Abruptly, Faith pushed herself back, away from the mirror. "You're right," she said. "They are ugly." She turned sideways on her chair and faced her sister. "I can't help you with your problem, Lexie, because honestly, I think it's too juvenile to even be called a real

11

problem. When you're in fourth grade, nothing that happens to you is a real problem."

Lexie snorted. "Oh, that's just dumb! When you were in fourth grade, you thought you had a million problems. I can still remember how you moaned and groaned about them all the time and made everybody in the house miserable!"

Faith turned back toward her reflection. "You're probably right," she said mournfully. "I may have taken them seriously back then. But that's only because I didn't know what middle school would be like . . . the kinds of problems I'd have to face . . . that enormous cafeteria, the crowded halls, the sadistic teachers, the exclusive cliques . . . or this horrible Sadie Hawkins thing . . . ." Her voice trailed off, and she frowned at her own face in the mirror.

"Who's Sadie Hawkins?" Ever since she'd started middle school, Faith had stopped going around with all her old friends from elementary school. Now her only so-called friend was a girl named Becky Brady. Lexie had never heard about anyone named Sadie before.

"It's not a *who*, it's a *what*. And, though I'd rather swallow rat poison than let Mom hear about it, I'll tell *you* that Sadie Hawkins is a living nightmare!"

Lexie snorted again. "Oh, will you give me a break? Everything that happens to you lately is a living nightmare! I guess it's really not all that surprising when you

12

think about it. You're so crabby, you turn everything into a bad dream—for everybody!"

Faith's face was starting to get red again. "Oh yeah?" she yelled. "Well, you'd be crabby, too, if you had to share a room with a little—"

Just then, the door to the room swung open, and Faith and Lexie's seventeen-year-old sister, Karen, burst in. As usual, Karen looked neat as a pin. Lexie was always amazed at how tidy her oldest sister was able to keep herself, no matter where she was or what she was doing. She wondered if Karen ran down to the laundry room to iron her clothes the minute she got home from school every day.

Karen waggled a finger at Faith and Lexie. "Are you little girls fighting *again?*" she scolded. "What *am* I going to do with the two of you?"

A sudden ominous silence filled the room. Then Faith spoke through tight lips. "We are not fighting, Karen," she said. "We are having a private discussion, with emphasis on the word *private.*"

"And what you can do with the two of us is *leave us alone!*" Lexie added.

Karen's face took on a wounded, holier-than-thou expression. She shook her head in resignation and disappointment and backed out into the hallway. Faith and Lexie knew she'd squeal on both of them for fighting and being rude the instant their mother came home from the university that afternoon.

13

"Thank you for stopping by, Karen!" Faith called after her. "But in the future when you come to call, would you mind knocking on the door for a change? It's the done thing in high society!"

Lexie giggled. It never failed. The one and only time she and Faith ever got along was when Karen tried to butt in on them and act like some kind of parent-in-training. "Can you believe her?" she said. "She always comes busting in here like our room is the hall closet, or something."

"Right. But if one of us *dared* to enter her royal highness's immaculate quarters without knocking . . ."

In matching throat-slitting motions, both girls drew the sides of their hands across their necks and made loud gurgling sounds. Lexie started to make another remark about Karen, but just then she caught sight of the time on her ankle watch again. Uh-oh! It was already four o'clock! The kids probably thought she was *dead* by now! Silently, she slid off the slick side of Faith's bed and sidled toward the door.

"If you're interested," Faith said, picking up her tweezers again, "I know what you can do about the talent show."

Lexie stopped in her tracks. "What?" she said eagerly.

"Pretend you're sick, of course! I mean, I would never do a thing like that, but it's right up your alley.

In fact, playing sick is another thing I've noticed you have a real talent for—particularly when you've lost your homework assignment or left your notebook at the park or have your usual trouble with your math problems."

Oops, Lexie thought. She'd thought she'd fooled the whole family with her dramatic flu attack last week, but as usual Faith had seen right through her. Without saying anything, she slipped through the doorway and out into the hall. Oh well, she thought. Even though Faith was her usual mean self, she had managed to come up with the one and only solution for the talent show problem. And though she'd been insulting, she'd been absolutely right about what she'd said. Lexie was good at faking illnesses, at least as far as her parents were concerned. She'd already gotten away with it twice since school started, and that was only three weeks ago!

She slid down the banister to the first floor, where she scurried through the empty kitchen and on out the back door into the yard. As she rounded the corner and picked up her bike in front of the house, she smiled to herself as she realized something. In spite of Faith's bad mood, the girl had done two extraordinary things that afternoon. Not only had she come up with the perfect way out of the talent show, she'd forgotten all about making her little sister clean up the bedroom!

TWO

The four girls bellowed with laughter as they lay in the warm grass. They were trying to play the ha ha stomach game, but they couldn't ever get past the first two people. Every time Suzy Frankowski put her fuzzy red head on Cheryl Ingebrettson's skinny stomach and tried to say, "Ha ha," she started shrieking with uncontrollable laughter. Suzy rolled around and screamed and laughed so hard she cracked up everyone else right along with her.

After a few more hysterical tries, they gave up on

the game and just lay there, talking and giggling in the middle of the unmowed field at the side of the baseball diamond. Debby Figenbaum turned up the volume on her transistor radio, and whenever they heard a song they knew, the four of them sang along, belting out the words and pretending they were rock stars. Suzy, who loved food, had brought along four boxes of Nerds, and they took turns pouring the little purple, pink, green, and yellow candies into each other's open mouths.

This is great, Lexie told herself. A perfect moment in my boring life. The weather felt warm and friendly, like the middle of summer, instead of the fourth week in September, and Lexie wished it could go on forever. As she rested on the squashed grass and hummed along with the chorus of an old Beatles song, she realized something for the first time. Next to Christmas morning, pepperoni pizza from Napoli's, and swimming at the lake, hanging out with the kids at the park ranked right up there as one of the best things in the world.

"Don't you think Stevie Crawford is cute?" Cheryl asked when the song was over.

Suzy immediately moaned, "Yeeessss," and Debby and Lexie shot each other a meaning-filled look through the blades of grass. Cheryl and Suzy were both madly in love with Stevie, just because he had straw-colored hair and giant blue eyes. But Debby and Lexie thought he was a rude, tongue-tied illiterate, and they silently wished the other two girls would stop gushing on about him all the time. Lately, Stevie Crawford seemed to be the only thing Cheryl and Suzy ever wanted to talk about, and it was getting pretty dull.

Also, it was a little upsetting because loving Stevie was the first thing in history that Debby, Lexie, Cheryl, and Suzy *hadn't* had in common. They'd all been in the same room at school every year since kindergarten, and in the same scout troop after school. They all lived near each other and went to day camp together every summer. They all liked the same kind of music, the same kind of clothes, the same kind of books, the same kind of movie stars, and the same kind of TV shows. They even liked the same kind of junk food.

But the best thing about them, Lexie thought, was that they all liked each other—and got along so well even though they were incredibly different kinds of people. Cheryl was sweet and considerate and thin, while Suzy was noisy and hot-tempered and chubby. Debby was worried and quiet and obedient, while Lexie was . . . well, to be honest, Lexie wasn't sure *what* she was, but the other kids seemed to like her, so she wasn't going to worry about it. She wasn't going to worry about stupid Stevie Crawford, either. The kids agreed about almost everything else besides him, even down to liking pizza flavored goldfish better than cheddar cheese flavored goldfish. And that was obviously more important.

"California Dreamin'," by the Mamas and Papas came on the radio, and the girls burst into song again. In the middle of a high note, Suzy sat up with a jerk. "Cheryl!" she said. "This would be the perfect song for us to lip-synch for the talent show!"

Cheryl nodded her head thoughtfully. "You're right," she said. "The parents would all like it because it's from their generation and everything."

Lexie turned her face sideways into the grass. *Lip-synching!* she thought. The perfect talent. Why didn't I think of that? Any moron can lip-synch! She rolled her face in the other direction and caught sight of Debby, gazing up into the sky. Debby was really Lexie's closest friend in the group, and by rights, the two of them should have been dreaming up an act they could do together. But the problem with that was that Debby didn't need to dream up an act. Debby had a built-in act because she actually had a real talent. She'd been taking piano lessons since she was three years old, and, at the age of nine, she already played like a pro. She practiced several hours a day and was always going off to play concerts with youth orchestras in other parts of the state. There was no way she'd want to team up with an untalented partner like Lexie.

As she thought about all of this, Suzy and Cheryl chattered excitedly about the show and what kind of costumes they'd wear. Then Debby tickled Lexie's leg with a blade of grass. "Do you know what you're doing for the show, Lexie?" she asked in her soft little voice.

"Uh . . . sure," Lexie mumbled. She wasn't really lying, she told herself. She did know what she was doing. It was all settled. She was getting sick! Still, she wished the kids would stop yammering on about the whole thing.

"So what are you going to do, Lex?" Suzy asked.

Holy moley, couldn't these girls ever let a subject drop? "Uh . . ." Lexie mumbled. "Uh . . . it's a secret." There was a moment of shocked silence as the other three swallowed this piece of news. It was obvious they could hardly believe their ears. The kids in the group told each other *everything*. They never kept secrets from each other!

All at once, Lexie felt really hot and uncomfortable. She sat up and brushed the grass out of her bushy brown hair and avoided looking at Debby's wounded expression. She decided she was being silly. These were her *friends* here, she told herself. They'd still like her, even if she didn't have a talent.

She was on the verge of a full confession, but just then, Suzy let out a whoop. "Is this watch on your ankle right, Lex?" she asked in horror.

"I think so." Lexie twisted her leg around so she could see the time. "Holy moley!" she exclaimed. "It's six o'clock!"

All at once, everyone was scrambling to get up, brush the grass off their shorts and T-shirts, and head for their bikes, parked over on the sidewalk near the park gate. Suzy and Cheryl shouted good-bye and drove off toward the west exit, while Debby and Lexie pedaled furiously up the Fiftieth Street hill toward home. When they reached Girard, Debby yelled, "Bye!" and made a sharp left turn. Lexie rode the last uphill block to Fremont all by herself.

As soon as she walked in the front door of her house, she knew she was in big trouble. Except for her brother, Daniel, who was almost never home anyway, the whole family was already sitting down to dinner. As usual, Karen was bubbling over about some fascinating thing that had happened in the high school library, where she worked during fifth period every afternoon. Mrs. Nielsen was asking Faith if she were absolutely positive she wanted a second helping of garlic bread, and Mr. Nielsen was describing a new camera lens he'd seen that day. But, when Lexie came in, everyone stopped talking at once. The four of them twisted around in their chairs and stared at her.

At last, Lexie's father broke the silence. "Lexie," he said sternly, "this is the third time you've been late for dinner this week."

"Sorry, Daddy." Lexie shuffled to the table and slid into her seat. As if the discussion were closed, she casually reached out to help herself from the big bowl of chili in the middle of the table. But her mother wasn't ready to let the subject drop.

"Lexie, honey," she said, "Daddy and I know you don't mean to be late so often. But I just want you to think about what kind of message you're sending to the rest of the family when you forget our feelings night after night. It's a message of not caring. Of not thinking of others' needs. Of lack of consideration."

Lexie stared down at her plate. "I *said* I was sorry, Mom," she said. And in her heart, she really was sorry. She wasn't trying to insult the whole family, for Pete's sake! She just couldn't ever seem to remember what time it was.

"Well, we appreciate the apology," her mother said, patting Lexie's hand. "And we won't talk about it anymore. For now."

Uh-oh, Lexie thought, as she picked up her fork. "For now." That didn't sound good. If she didn't do something fast, her mother might decide to hold a rap session on incurable lateness!

She searched her mind for a new subject, any subject, that would wipe the topic of lateness right out of her mother's mind, but she just couldn't think of a thing. True, she could always ask Karen how many books she'd reshelved at the library that day. Karen absolutely loved her job at the high school library. In fact, she loved everything about high school, just as she'd loved junior high school and elementary school before that. Lexie thought her oldest sister was crazy, but the truth was that she was secretly jealous of Karen's love for school—and the ease with which Karen always got straight A's on her report card. Lexie didn't know how Karen managed to be so perfectly good all the time. What would it be like to actually *want* to leap out of bed on Monday mornings because you just couldn't wait to run to school and hit the books?

Anyway, Karen was almost always willing to bubble on about whatever it was she'd done at the library that day, so Lexie knew she could count on her to provide a new topic of conversation. But was it worth the price? Karen's detailed, chatty library stories were so boring they seemed to suck all the taste right out of the food! Still, if it would take their mother's mind off Lexie. . . .

She'd turned toward Karen and opened her mouth to speak when her father saved the day. At the head of the table, Mr. Nielsen cleared his throat and spread his hands wide. "I have a nickel in my back pocket," he said, "for the first person who can guess the answer to the riddle I heard today."

Everyone at the table kept right on eating and drinking, except for Lexie, who put down her fork and looked up expectantly. She won the riddle nickel almost every single night, though of course she realized it didn't mean all that much, since almost no one else even bothered to try to guess the answer anymore. But Lexie didn't care about that. No matter what the rest of the family thought, she believed her father's corny old riddles were really funny. And she loved trying to figure out what silly pun would show up in the answer.

Tonight Lexie particularly wanted to guess the riddle because she was trying to improve her record. This week she'd only guessed one out of two, and Monday's riddle had been so easy it almost didn't count. "What reindeer would you find in your kitchen sink?" her father had asked that night. Lexie had raced through a mental list of Santa's reindeer and shouted, "Comet!" before any-one else had time to breathe. Everyone had laughed, but Lexie had asked for a harder one the next time, and her father had promised to come up with a real brain stomper.

It had taken him two days to think of one, but he'd finally done it. On Wednesday, he'd asked, "What shape is a kiss?" At first, Lexie had thought she'd guess the answer right away. But after she'd run through every single shape she could think of from rectangular to trap-ezoidal, she'd known she was in trouble. She'd been just about to give up when, to her amazement, her brother, Daniel, had looked up from his chicken drum-stick and quietly said, "El*lip*tical." The whole family had stopped eating and stared at him in wonder. On the rare occasions when Daniel was home for dinner, he almost never took part in the conversation, and he certainly never played the riddle game! But now he'd come up with a truly difficult answer without even batting an eye!

Typical, Lexie thought now. Daniel had become the champion of almost everything he'd ever tried to do, and he could probably guess the riddle every single night if he felt like it. But tonight he wasn't even home yet, so Lexie had a clear field. She sat forward in her chair, ready to hear the latest riddle. "What's the difference," her father was saying, "between *here* and *there?*"

Lexie leaned back and started thinking hard. "What's the Difference" riddles could be pretty difficult, but she could usually get the answer if she could figure out the trick. She was toying around with the two words when Faith spoke up.

"Do we really have to go through with this babyish riddle charade every single night?" she asked shrilly.

Expressions of shock and dismay appeared on each face at the table. Except for Lexie, who was lost in concentration, everyone in the room gaped at Faith in surprise. The Nielsens had played the riddle game almost every night since the beginning of time! It was a family tradition. To be sure, most of the family thought it was pretty silly, but Mr. Nielsen got such a kick out of it, no one had ever thought of complaining about it before.

Mrs. Nielsen was looking at Faith with an anxious, concerned expression, but Mr. Nielsen's face resembled a kicked puppy's. "Why, Faith," he said slowly. "I thought you enjoyed the riddle game. You always used to be the best guesser."

Faith wasn't showing any mercy. "That's just it, Daddy," she said. "I *used to* enjoy it! When I was a little kid!"

At that moment, the switch clicked on in Lexie's head. "The difference between *here* and *there* is," she cried triumphantly, "the letter *t!* See, *there* has a *t* at the beginning and *here* doesn't!"

On a normal night, the whole family always made a big deal of laughing and applauding when somebody guessed the riddle, particularly a tricky one like that. But tonight, Lexie's answer was greeted with an uncomfortable silence as everyone looked down at their hands, trying to avoid Mr. Nielsen's eyes. Lexie stared around the table in confusion, until her glance came to rest on Faith's angry, puckered face. Immediately, she sensed what was going on.

Well, that just figures! Lexie said to herself. Faith is taking the fun out of everything around here, and now she's wrecked the riddle game! Lexie wanted to jump up and sock her sister right in the nose. But all at once, she thought of an even better way of getting even.

26

"You don't look very happy tonight, Faith," she said sweetly. "What's the matter? Could it be that you're upset about . . . oh, I don't know . . . say . . . Sadie Hawkins?"

Karen gave a squeal of excitement, and cried, "Oh, a Sadie Hawkins, how exciting!" Faith took a sharp breath and shot an anxious glance at the foot of the table, obviously hoping her mother hadn't heard. But the damage had been done. Mom put down her fork and directed the full blast of her complete, undivided attention at Faith.

"What's this, Faith?" she asked eagerly. "Are they having a Sadie Hawkins dance at the middle school?" She was always saying how good it would be for Faith to join more clubs and get involved in more extracurricular activities. She just couldn't understand why Faith seemed unhappy so much of the time and wasn't always bringing crowds of friends home and begging to have parties every night, the way Karen had when she was thirteen.

Faith glared at Lexie and mumbled something unintelligible to her mother.

Mrs. Nielsen looked more and more interested. "I'll interpret that mumble as a yes, Faith. When is the dance, dear?"

"Two weeks from last Saturday," Faith muttered.

"Well, have you thought about whom you might want to invite?"

Faith looked ready to cry, but Lexie couldn't figure out what was going on. She'd thought Sadie Hawkins was some stupid friend of Becky Brady's that Faith wanted to be friends with, or something, and now it turned out she—*it*—was a dance. But why did Faith have to ask a boy to go with her? "Wait a minute!" Lexie interrupted. "I thought the boys usually had to ask the girls to go to a dance with them."

"That usually is the case," her father explained. "But in a Sadie Hawkins dance, the tables are turned. The girls get to do the honors."

"It's a lovely idea, really." Mrs. Nielsen was in high, enthusiastic gear now. "A good opportunity for the boys and girls to get to know one another at the beginning of the year. It's a terrific way for some of the more shy, less outgoing girls," she turned toward Faith, "like you, dear, to make some new friends."

Lexie swallowed hard and tried not to look at the stricken face across the table from her. What had she done? She'd wanted to get even with her sister, but she hadn't meant to throw her to the wolves like this! She fervently wished she could untell everybody about the stupid Sadie Hawkins thing, but one look at her mother's happy, gung-ho expression told her there was no going back. For the next two weeks, Faith would be encouraged, cajoled, teased, and coaxed to call up some dumb boy and ask him to the dance. She would suffer

28

through every single minute of it. And she would make Lexie suffer right along with her.

In fact, Faith's revenge was already beginning. "While we're all on the subject of extracurricular activities, Lexie *dear,* why don't you tell Mom and Daddy about the big scout project you're looking forward to so much it's making you simply *sick* with anticipation?"

Lexie grimaced, but before her parents could shift their focus to her, she was saved by the arrival of her brother, Daniel. With a bang of the front door, he stomped into the house and dropped his dirty, smelly sweatshirt right in the middle of the living room. Then, with his cleats clicking noisily across the hardwood floor, he came over to the table and thumped down in the empty chair next to Faith's.

As Daniel scraped the rest of the contents of the chili bowl onto his plate, Lexie looked around the room in disbelief. When no one said anything, she banged her hand down on the table to attract attention. "I can't believe this!" she said when everyone was staring at her. "I come home ten minutes late, and I'm treated like a mass murderer! But Daniel bops through the door at least half an hour late, and no one even bats an eye!"

There was a short, shocked silence. Then her father turned to look at her. "Daniel has soccer practice on Monday afternoon, Lexie." As if that explained everything.

"Well, should we kiss his feet now or later?" Lexie muttered under her breath. But she didn't say anything out loud. What was the point? Daniel got away with murder around here, just because he was the only boy. Lexie knew for a fact that soccer practice was over by 5:30, and here it was 6:30, and he was just getting home. But did anybody lecture him about not caring, disrespect, and lack of consideration? No way! Everybody acted like it was a positive privilege to be in the same room with his sweaty, jocky, fifteen-year-old body!

Even now, her father was asking Daniel to describe the plays Coach Higgins had run that day, and her mother and Karen were both leaning forward in their chairs, simply dying to hear the answer. For the moment, everybody's attention was fixed on the son of the house.

Well, Lexie thought, at least Daniel's coming home had accomplished one thing. It had saved her from having to tell everybody what the big scout project was. It wasn't likely, but there was an infinitesimal chance her parents might forget to ask about it later on.

As she scooped up her last bite of chili, Lexie glanced around the dinner table and saw that the entire family was still hanging on Daniel's every word. The entire family, that is, with the exception of Faith. She was staring across the table, glowering at her little sister. And there was murder in her eyes.

30

Three

"What's an inky pinky for a silly rabbit?"

"Oh, give me a break, Daddy!" Lexie said. "That's too easy. In fact, I think I made up funny bunny myself when I was five years old! Ask me a hard one."

Mr. Nielsen gripped the steering wheel and frowned in thought, while Lexie gazed out the window and busily counted the cows on her side of the road. It was Saturday morning, and even though it was October third, the weather was still as warm and sunny as the middle of July. When her father had suggested an outing to

31

River Road, Lexie had eagerly accepted. River Road was one of her favorite places on earth. When she was tiny, the whole Nielsen famly had gone on an expedition there almost every month. But as time went on, Karen and Daniel gradually became busier and busier with their own activities, and one by one, they each stopped coming on the trips. For several years after that, Mr. and Mrs. Nielsen kept on going with just Faith and Lexie. But then last fall, Mrs. Nielsen had gotten so bogged down with schoolwork, she'd become too busy to do almost *anything* but study and write papers.

Now, in spite of Lexie's weekly begging and pleading, it had been almost a whole year since anyone in the family had gone to River Road. Today, though, Lexie's father had finally had a free Saturday morning and had offered to make the trip. At the moment, the two of them were sitting in the front seat, playing their favorite driving game, cow countdown.

"I've got one you'll never guess," Mr. Nielsen said with his best devilish grin. "What's an inkedy pinkedy for an evil preacher?"

"Hmmmm," Lexie said. She thought for a minute. The synonym for preacher was almost certain to be minister. So what was a word that rhymed with minister and meant evil? "Aha!" she yelled. "Sinister minister!"

Her father laughed and slapped the wheel with delight. "I'll tell you, Lexerino," he said. "You're getting to be impossible to stump."

32

Lexie looked out at the passing scenery and grinned at the compliment. Her grin grew even wider when she saw a field full of horses on her side of the road. "White horse on my side, Daddy!" she yelled happily. "I get to double my points!"

Her happiness faded at once when she heard a loud, gusty sigh coming from the seat behind her. At the same instant, they passed a cemetery on her side of the road, which automatically wiped out her entire cow score. Bitterly, she twisted around to look over her shoulder. A gloomy, glum-faced Faith sat hunched down in the corner of the backseat, her exhausted head resting against the side window. As Lexie watched her, Faith pulled a smuggled bag of Reeses Pieces out of her pocket and popped one into her mouth.

For the hundredth time that morning, Lexie wished Faith had stayed home. Of course that's exactly what Faith had begged and pleaded to do. But Mom had said she'd heard enough moping and groaning around the house to last a lifetime during the last week, and a Saturday morning drive to the countryside would do Faith a world of good. So she'd insisted that Faith go along with Lexie and Daddy. And now here she was, moping and groaning around the backseat of the car. And sighing, *always* sighing.

Lexie turned around and faced frontward again, but her mind was still on her sister. What in the world is bugging Faith these days, anyway? she asked herself.

She used to love going to River Road. She used to beg to go there even harder than she begged to stay home this morning!

Sorrowfully, Lexie thought back on all the games she and her sister used to play before Faith became such a creep. Which wasn't to say they hadn't always fought like cats and dogs. But in-between fights they and their friends had played Monopoly and superheroes and cops and robbers and ant circus and paper doll hospital and dollhouse and stuffed animal wedding. . . . Thinking of stuffed animal wedding made Lexie think of Faith's Bananny bear, stuffed away in a bag in the closet, and she suddenly felt overcome with confusion and anger. All at once, she wanted to take her sister by the shoulders and shake some sense into her. But before she could vault over the backseat, she realized her father was speaking to her again.

"Help me watch for the turn, will you, Lexerino? You know I always shoot past it."

"It's right there, Daddy," Faith said with a weary wave of her hand. "Right after that Best Western billboard."

Mr. Nielsen slowed down and turned left onto the bumpy, dusty, unpaved, almost always empty River Road. Lexie felt her pulse rate quicken with excitement as she sat forward to look out the window. River Road was the most beautiful place in the world. On one side

34

of the road was a thick, marshy forest, where the leaves were already starting to turn bright red and yellow. Her father referred to it as a "slough," and liked to tromp through in it for hours at a time, lugging his binoculars, camera, and tripod and taking endless, painstaking pictures of flowers and birds.

But Lexie preferred the other side of the road, which was really just a big, open hill, half woods and half grassy fields. The fields were perfect for running and jumping and rolling on, and the woods were perfect for hiding and climbing and collecting things, but neither one was Lexie's favorite place. Her favorite place was at the top of the hill. She could hardly wait to get there.

The instant her father stopped the car, Lexie opened her door and jumped out. "Come on, Faith!" she yelled. "I'll race you to the thicket."

Faith rolled down her window and sighed. "I think I'll just stay here and read," she said, resting her head on her arms.

Mr. Nielsen rolled his eyes and shook his head. "No dice, honey," he said. "It's just too beautiful an Indian summer day to spend roasting in the backseat of a car. Everybody out. I'll meet you girls back here in one hour. Let's synchronize our watches. Mine says ten thirty-two A.M., central daylight time."

Lexie grabbed her ankle and hopped around on one foot until she could read her watch. "That's what mine says, too, Daddy. See you later." She started across the road toward the hill, but she remembered something and came running back. She reached into the front seat and took a long, brown bag from the floor. Then she ran across the road to the hill again.

With another long, mournful sigh, Faith got out of the car and slowly, slowly, trailed after her sister. By the time she'd dragged herself to the thicket at the top of the hill, Lexie had already been there impatiently waiting for ten minutes.

"Look, Faith!" she said excitedly. "It's just like it used to be, all divided up into different parts. Remember? It looks just like a real house! We said this part was the bedroom, and this part was the living room, and this part was the kitchen." As she spoke, she darted in and out through the thorny, leafy branches. "We used rocks and sticks and stuff and said they were pots and spoons, and we set up a whole dinner table, remember?"

Faith brushed some leaves off the top of a large, flat rock near the entrance to the thicket. She sat down and watched in silence as her sister picked up a long, leafy stick and painstakingly swept out the sticks and leaves from the thicket floor. She still wasn't speaking when Lexie started erecting an elaborate kitchen stove out of rocks, twigs, and mud. After about twenty minutes, though, Lexie suddenly seemed to realize that her companion hadn't said a single word since they'd arrived.

Exasperated, she came over and planted herself, filthy hands on hips, right in front of her sister's rock.

"Are you sick or something, Faith?" she asked.

"I guess you might put it that way," Faith answered. "I'm certainly sick of Mom following me around all week, trying to rap with me about the Sadie Hawkins dance. It wouldn't be so bad if I didn't know that what she's saying is right—that I really would like to go to the dance if I could. But I can't, and that's that, so I wish she'd just lay off with her gentle but firm expressions of concerned, constructive criticism. But she won't, and it's all the fault of your big, fat, blabbering mouth."

Lexie didn't like being called a blabbermouth, but, in spite of that, she felt a pang of sympathy for her sister. In fact, she'd been feeling sorry for her all week. Mom had been unbelievably dedicated to her help-Faith-realize-it's-in-her-own-best-interests-to-go-to-the-dance campaign. Every time Faith so much as sat down, Mom put an arm around her and asked her to try to define why she *really* felt so much threatening negativity about the dance. Mrs. Nielsen had applied every single technique she'd learned in counseling class in the last seven months, as well as every known form of subtle and not-so-subtle parental pressure. But in the face of all of it, Faith had still stubbornly insisted she'd rather die than invite a boy to the Sadie Hawkins.

Even though she couldn't stand her sister's moodiness

and bad temper, Lexie had to admire her guts. Still, she couldn't help feeling Faith was making life a lot harder than was necessary. "If you really want to go to the dance, why don't you just go ahead and call some boy and invite him?" Lexie asked her now. "Why don't you call that guy what's-his-name that you and Becky Brady are always whispering about on the phone?"

"His *name* is Justin Dupree! But I can't just call him up, just like that."

"Why not?"

"Because," Faith began. "Because . . . I'm so . . . and he's so . . . and what if he . . . ?" She threw out her hands in frustration. "Oh, what am I trying to explain this stuff to an ignorant little simpleton like you for?" She glanced around the thicket. "Why don't you just . . . go off and play with whatever it is you have in that bag you've been carting around?"

"That's the first good idea you've had in about a year, Faith." Lexie picked up the bag and pulled out the pieces to a big red box kite. Her grandmother had sent it to her for her birthday last April, but she'd never had a chance to use it until now. Today seemed like the perfect day for its maiden voyage.

If she could ever get it together, that is. She studied the directions for thirty seconds and then began fiddling around with the pieces, trying to put notch A into slot B. Before long, she threw the directions on the ground and shrugged. "I give up," she said. "Nothing fits to-gether. I think they must have left out a piece or some-thing."

Faith snorted and got to her feet. "Leave it to Lexie," she said disgustedly. "Give up on it before you even get started." She hunched down on the ground and picked up the instruction sheet. In less than ten minutes, she had the entire kite assembled.

She got up again and handed the kite to her sister. "Go out and see if you can fly it, Lexie," she said.

Lexie reached out for the kite. Then she changed her mind. "You fly it, Faith. You're the one who put it together."

Faith gave a careless shrug, but she carried the kite out of the thicket and on into the open field. When she was far enough away from the trees, she held the bright red paper and wood box high up above her head. Then she let go and started racing through the tall grass.

Almost at once, a breeze caught the kite and lifted it up into the air. Faith let out more and more string, and the kite rose and rose. Within minutes, it had be-come a tiny red square speck high above them in the blue sky.

Yelling and shrieking, Lexie ran to her sister's side. "That was unbelievable, Faith! You're the wizard of kites! The thing just shot right up there like a great big red bat or something!"

Faith laughed and pointed to the string. "Look how the string's twanging and jerking," she said. "The wind must be really powerful up there."

Lexie looked at the string and then up at her sister's animated face. Faith's thick brown hair was blowing backward in the breeze, and her cheeks were red from the wind and the running. Her gray-blue eyes were shiny and excited.

Holy moley! Lexie thought. Will wonders never cease? Faith is happy! She's actually enjoying herself!

All at once, Lexie felt so good she wanted to stay on the hilltop forever, watching her sister fly the kite. For several long moments, she stood motionless by Faith's side, staring up at the little red square bobbing around high up in the blue sky. But finally, she couldn't stand it. "Hey!" she said, reaching out for the string. "Do I ever get a turn?"

Faith gazed up at the kite as if she hadn't heard what Lexie had said. Then she seemed to shake herself and come back down to earth. "Oh, all right," she said. She handed over the reel of string. "Just hold on tight or the wind will pull it right away from you."

Lexie grabbed the string, and, for a few more minutes, the two girls stood on the hillside, staring up at the sky. Then the beep of a honking car horn sounded from the road below. At first, they both ignored it. But then the horn beeped again.

"That must be Daddy," Faith said. "We'd better go."

"That *can't* be Daddy! We haven't even been here a whole hour yet. And that would mean he's early. But he's *never* early when he's taking bird pictures!"

"Well, he is this time. Let's go!"

"He can wait a few minutes. I mean, after all, he always keeps us waiting, and . . ."

"I'm going!" Faith announced. She marched off down the side of the hill without another word.

"Leave it to Faith to be Miss Perfect," Lexie said out loud. The car horn honked again, and she decided it really was her father and she'd better bring in the kite. She turned the reel of string in her hands, but the kite was pulling so hard, the reel barely moved. The kite didn't want the day to end, either!

Slowly, Lexie wound the string around the reel again. She made some progress, but it took forever. By the time the kite had come down close to the tops of some nearby trees, her finger muscles were aching and tired. Why did Faith have to leave her alone up here to do all the hard work?

She wound the string a few more times, and the kite barely seemed to move. At last, sick of the tedious twisting and turning, Lexie decided to try to get all of the kite line in at once. She reached out, grabbed the string, and hauled it in with one powerful yank. The bright red box bobbed and dipped once against the blue sky. Then, without warning, it turned upside down and sky-dived straight downward at top speed.

Frantically, Lexie tried to let out more string. But it was no use. It was too late. The kite kept right on plummeting. It was doomed, and there was nothing anyone could do.

Faith's voice in her ear made her jump. "Lexie, Daddy sent me back up to find out what you're . . ." She stopped talking the instant she spotted the kite on its sickening downward spiral. *Crrracck!* The kite slammed into the top of the thicket and splintered into a million pieces.

Faith's sigh was so loud it seemed to shake the hillside. "Oh, what's the use, Lexie?" she said. "You ruin everything you touch!"

As Lexie watched her sister stomp back down the hillside, she blinked back hot, self-pitying tears. "You're wrong about that, Faith!" she yelled after her. "*You're* the one who ruins everything!"

Four

That night, Lexie lay in her bed, waiting for her father to say good night and drowsily half-dreaming about her performance at the scouts' talent show. In her fantasy, she gave up the idea of playing sick and then somehow magically learned all there was to know about ballet the night before the show. She appeared on stage in a sparkling diamond-studded tutu. Her graceful leaps and twirls were so incredible, so truly remarkable, that the agent from the American Ballet Company, who happened to be in the audience, immediately implored her to come to New York to join the troupe. Lexie's parents and brother and sisters were, naturally enough, overcome with joy, pride, and shame for all the mean things they'd ever done to their darling, talented daughter and sister. They were down on their knees, sobbing and begging for forgiveness, when Lexie's father finally snapped on the hall light and came up the stairs to say good night.

He stood quietly for a minute, silhouetted in the doorway, listening to hear if the girls were already snoring.

"We're awake, Daddy," Faith called from her bed. "At least I am."

"So am I," chimed in Lexie.

Without turning on their light, Mr. Nielsen stepped into the room, immediately stubbing his toe on the box containing Lexie's rock collection. "Yowch!" he yelled. He picked up his foot and hobbled over to sit down on the corner of Faith's bed.

"I hope you're satisfied, Lexie," Faith said. "I knew somebody was going to get injured in here one day. Now, Daddy, maybe you and Mom will understand the kind of living conditions I have to put up with all the time."

"Oh, just shut up, Faith," Lexie began, sitting up in her bed. "Why do you always have to be such a goody-goody and—"

44

"Why don't you both shut up?" their father snapped, still rubbing his sore toe. Then, realizing how childish he'd sounded, he cleared his throat and tried again. "What I mean to say is, let's not make the usual federal case out of this, all right? Every single thing that happens in this house doesn't *have* to be a reason for you two girls to start fighting!"

"Tell that to Faith," Lexie began. "She's always—"

"Lexie!" Mr. Nielsen's voice was unusually sharp. "That's enough!"

The three of them sat in silence for a few minutes. Then Mr. Nielsen peered at the fluorescent numbers on his watch. "It's getting pretty late, so I'll just say good night and don't let the bedbugs bite. . . ."

"And sleep tight till morning light, all right?" Lexie finished.

"All right!" Their father started out of the room, but Faith called him back. "Daddy," she said, "would you please, please, *please* remember to turn the hall light back off when you get downstairs?"

Mr. Nielsen's face looked surprised. "Well, of course, Faith. Why wouldn't I?"

"Well, because you forget almost every single night, and then it shines right in here into our eyes, and one of us has to get up and turn it off."

"Have you ever considered simply closing the door to your room?" her father asked.

"I've considered it," Faith snapped. "But *she* won't!"

There was a short silence. "With the door closed," Lexie explained in a small voice, "I feel like there won't be enough air in here. I'm afraid I'll suffocate."

Faith snorted, but Mr. Nielsen nodded his head as if this fear were completely sensible. "Okay," he said. "I'll leave the door open."

"And you'll remember the light?" Faith asked again.

"Right. Tonight I'll make a special effort to remember."

He left the room, and the girls listened to his footsteps as he walked along the hall and on down the stairs. There followed a moment of tense, silent waiting.

"Five, four, three, two, one . . ." Faith counted. "That's it! He's gone into the living room without turning off the light down there. He forgot again!"

"Well, I'm not getting up again tonight. It's your turn."

"It is not! I distinctly remember getting out of my warm, snuggly bed last night, running across the freezing floor, turning out the light, cracking my leg on your roller skate, and falling back into bed."

"Well, I don't care if it *is* my turn. I'm not getting up."

Faith sighed and threw back her covers. "As usual," she said, "I'm stuck with being the responsible one." She hurried across the room, snapped the upstairs switch outside their door, and hurried back into her bed.

After that both girls lay quietly in the darkness, thinking their own separate thoughts. Before long, their eyes closed and they drifted off to sleep. Ten minutes later, they were awakened by a series of loud, banging *thud-a-thuds!* that seemed to shake the foundations of the whole house.

"I can't believe it!" Lexie said as her eyes shot open. "He's doing it again."

"Why does he need to kick his soccer ball around his room like that? He practically lives with the thing all day long as it is!"

Gratefully, they heard their father's voice shouting up the stairs for Daniel to knock it off with the ball. Pleased that for once their sacred brother had gotten yelled at, the two girls nestled down in their beds again. Lexie was partway into a dream about swimming all the way across Lake Harriet in front of an admiring, cheering crowd, when the hall light came on again, hitting her right between the eyes. Then Karen's laughing, annoyingly cheery voice sounded only a few yards away from the door.

"It was the funniest thing!" their sister bellowed back down the stairs to her parents. "The girl who works during fourth period had filed all the titles starting with the *word A* under the *letter A*. Can you imagine? I was laughing so hard, I could hardly see what I was doing while I was refiling them!"

"Ha, ha, hardy har," Lexie said dryly.

"Why can't she ever say what's on her mind while she's actually in the same room with Mom and Daddy?" Faith asked the darkness. "Why does she always have to tramp all the way up here and then screech it back down the stairs like that?"

"You know what's going to happen next, don't you?"

"Karen!" Faith screamed at the top of her lungs. "Don't go into your room without turning off the"— they both heard the sound of Karen's bedroom door closing—"light," Faith finished weakly.

"She can't hear you with the door closed," Lexie said.

"Particularly when she's singing opera to herself like that."

"If you can call that singing."

The girls lay quietly listening and suffering while Karen strained to sing a series of high tra la, la, la's. When their sister hit six shriekingly sharp notes in a row, they both went into a long howling fit of giggles at the exact same instant.

"I'm surprised all the dogs in the neighborhood don't come running to our house!" Lexie gasped when she could speak.

Faith barked out a laugh and sat up in her bed to

wipe her eyes. "No one else in the world would believe what we have to go through every night just to get to sleep! She sounds just like a . . ."

"Faith!" Lexie interrupted. "Look at the wall! Over your bed."

Faith twisted around to look where Lexie was pointing. The moon was shining right in through the window and illuminating her whole corner of the room. The combination of the pale light and the shifting shadows of the trees outside made an eerie, moving shape on the wall.

"Uh-huh," Faith said. She yawned and started to lie back down.

"Don't you get it?" Lexie said excitedly. "It's a perfect alien moonbeam from outer space!" She started talking in a mechanical, robotlike voice. "I am Alien Moonbeam Number Eight Six Two. I have come to your room to study your life forms. Please allow me to moonbeam you onto my space vessel immediately."

Faith's sigh was so loud, Lexie was sure she felt the breeze all the way over in her bed. "Listen, Lexie," she said. "There's something I keep trying to drum into your head. I'm too old to play stuff like moonbeam alien from outer space! I'm too old for dolls and make-believe and all those things. I mean, what if Becky Brady or any of the other kids found out Barb and Kathy and I were still playing witches and goblins with you and Debby last summer? I'd be the laughingstock of the whole school!"

Lexie lay in her bed in shocked silence. When she finally spoke, her voice was small and quiet. "Are you too old for the dollhouse, too?" she asked. She felt as if she could stand anything if Faith would just say she'd still play with the dollhouse. Their grandmother had given it to them when Lexie was three and Faith was seven, and they'd spent entire days at a time making the furniture and dishes out of things like bottle caps and match boxes. Sometimes Lexie liked to pretend the family that lived in the dollhouse was real, and that at night they came to life and ran around and used all the things the girls had made for them.

Faith was quiet for so long, Lexie began to wonder whether the older girl had fallen asleep. But at last she spoke. "I'm too old for the dollhouse, too," she said. "You can have all my people and their furniture, too."

Without saying a word, Lexie turned over on her stomach and started to cry. She didn't make a sound, but the hot, painful tears poured out of her eyes until her pillow was a wet, soggy mess. Lexie didn't even notice. All she could think about was that she would never *ever* play with the dollhouse again.

Five

The next afternoon, Lexie let Cheryl Ingebrettson and Suzy Frankowski in through the kitchen door. The three of them headed directly toward the basement. When they were halfway down the steps, they stopped for a minute to listen to Debby Figenbaum, who was already downstairs playing the "Moonlight Sonata" on the Nielsens' banged-up old upright piano.

"Wow," Cheryl whispered. "I hope Debby is going to play that for the talent show. Just think how good that would sound on a *decent* piano!"

"Well, excuse me," Lexie whispered back. "Just because *my* family can't afford a baby grand . . ."

Debby heard their voices, and the music stopped abruptly. "Did you bring all your stuff with you, Suzy and Cheryl?" she called up the stairs.

"What stuff?" Lexie asked. For the first time, she noticed that Suzy and Cheryl were each carrying several bulging plastic trash bags. "What are all those things for?"

"It's some of my mom's fabric and thread and junk," Suzy explained. "We thought we'd all work on our costumes for the talent show this afternoon. I even brought all my father's old Mamas and Papas albums so we can copy their clothes right off the covers."

"And we can listen to their music while we work," Cheryl added. "For inspiration."

"I thought we were going to play Space Quest on the computer today," Lexie said with a frown. Why hadn't Debby told her they were going to work on their costumes? What would happen if her mother came downstairs and asked what they were doing? Ever since Faith had blabbed about the show last week, Lexie had been waiting for her mother to ask about it, but so far no one had even mentioned it. Lexie was beginning to hope she could get away without even telling her parents about the stupid thing!

"Oh, we'll probably have time for a quick game of

Space Quest, too," Cheryl was saying in her cheery way. "The costumes won't take all that long."

"But what about Debby?" Lexie asked. "What's she supposed to do all afternoon? She doesn't need a costume to play the piano!"

"Well, actually, I *do,*" Debby said shyly. "I'm so sick of playing Beethoven for every single recital and show, I decided to do something different this time. I'm going to dress up like Elton John or Liberace or somebody— you know, with sequins and rhinestones and satin, or something, and then stand up and jump around while I play."

Cheryl and Suzy both yelled with delight. "That's fantastic, Deb!" Suzy said.

Lexie frowned again. "Are you sure a far-out rock show type of thing will be all right with Mrs. Noble? I mean, this *is* the Girl Scouts we're talking here, Debby!"

Debby's face was surprised and anxious. "Well, I think it'll be okay. I mean, Mrs. Noble said the show was supposed to be fun, so I just assumed . . ." Her voice trailed off, and she frowned.

"Of course it'll be okay, Debby!" Suzy said. "It'll be the hit of the show!" Behind Debby's back, she shot Lexie an angry "are you nuts?" kind of look.

"What kind of costume will you be making for the talent show, Lex?" Cheryl asked quickly. She was always the one who tried to head off any kind of disagreement in the group.

"Uh . . ." Lexie stalled. "Ummm . . ." Then, all at once, her words came out in a rush. "Well, that's just the point, isn't it? I don't need a costume for what I'm doing. So I guess you guys lugged all that stuff over here for nothing!"

The other three girls stared at Lexie in surprise as her angry words bounced and boomeranged off the fake-wood-paneled walls. "What exactly did you say you'd be doing in the show again, Lexie?" Suzy asked after a minute.

All at once, Lexie knew why no one had told her about this afternoon's costume project. They were trying to trick her into saying what she was planning to do. They'd been bugging her about it off and on for days. They acted like they were obsessed with the show, or something. Cheryl and Suzy had hardly even mentioned Stevie Crawford all week!

Couldn't they figure out that Lexie just didn't want to talk about it? She forced her voice to sound calm. "I told you guys before," she said. "What I'm doing for the show is a secret."

"A secret that doesn't need a costume," Suzy said irritably.

"Right," Lexie snapped.

Cheryl the peacemaker stepped in again. "Well, I can hardly wait to see what you're going to do, Lexie,"

54

she said. "But, you know, if it doesn't work out, you can always join up with me and Suzy and lip-synch along with us."

Suzy looked surprised, but then, after a few seconds, she grinned. "Good idea!" she said. "That would be terrific. You could be one of the Papas!"

Lexie swallowed hard. That's what was so great about the kids, she told herself. They backed you up even when you were acting like a total slime. She was positive Cheryl had figured out that Lexie didn't have a clue what to do for the show, but Cheryl was so sweet she'd never try to force a person to admit an embarrassing thing like that. Instead, she was offering a face-saving way out.

But, desperate and left out as she felt, Lexie didn't want to be included in the other kids' plans just because they felt sorry for their untalented friend. She made herself smile at Cheryl and Suzy. "Thanks a lot, you two," she said nonchalantly, "but, since the group wasn't called the Mamas and *Papa,* I think three of us would look pretty dumb up there. But, anyway, I do have an idea about what we can do this afternoon. While I don't need anything to wear for the talent show, I do need to make an outfit for Halloween, which you'll note if you'll check out your calendars, is only a few short weeks away. Why don't I work on that while you're working on your costumes?"

Everyone agreed that that was an excellent idea, and,

within minutes, the green-and-white speckled linoleum floor was covered with the contents of the two garbage bags. Suzy's mother was part-owner of a fabric store, so Suzy had been able to bring piles and piles of fabric samples, spools of thread, balls of yarn, and containers of sequins, beads, rhinestones. Cheryl had brought two big bottles of glue and several cans of wild-colored spray paint.

While Debby put the Mamas and Papas record on the stereo, the other girls started working on their creations. Lexie went to the old clothes trunk in the laundry room and began rummaging around. She was planning to be a female vampire for Halloween, so all she had to do was haul out her mother's ancient black velvet floor-length evening cloak from her college sorority days. Actually, the cloak didn't need many changes to make it look exactly like a vampire's cape. The main problem was that it was about six inches too long. Lexie made a fat, uneven fold all along the bottom of the cloak, planted herself in the middle of the floor, and started sewing in a hem with huge crooked black stitches.

"That hem you're sewing reminds me of a really great rut-i-dut-dut-lut-e I've been saving to tell you, Lex," Suzy said after a while. "And I don't think even you will be able to guess the answer."

The other three girls immediately translated the Ut language word into standard English. Minus the *uts*

56

after the consonants, rut-i-dut-dut-lut-e meant 'riddle.'

"O-kut-a-yut!" said Lexie. "Fire away."

"O-kut-a-yut. Here it is: Why are surgeons always so happy?"

Lexie concentrated on her next inch-long stitch, and the answer leaped into her brain. "Because their work always keeps them in stitches?"

"The Amazing Lexie!" Suzy said while Debby and Cheryl laughed out loud. Then Debby happened to glance over at Lexie's cape.

"Lexie!" she cried in horror, crawling away from the pile of rhinestones she was gluing onto her brother's Minnesota Twins jacket. "That's not how you make a hem. You're supposed to make tiny stitches on the inside that won't show up on the outside. And anyway, that hem's all bunched up and crooked. If you'll stand up on a chair, I'll be happy to pin it up for you, and—"

"Finished!" cried Lexie, triumphantly holding up the shortened cape. "Who cares if it doesn't look perfect? It only has to last for one night's worth of trick-or-treating. And besides, it's dark outside on Halloween, so no one will notice if it's a little uneven."

"Well, when you catch your foot in it and trip and fall into the path of an oncoming car," Debby said, scuttling back over to her jacket, "don't come crawling to me!"

"I probably won't be able to crawl if I've been

squashed by a car," Lexie said. "So you don't have to worry."

She put on the cape, made her hands into two rigid, grasping claws, and pretended to suck blood from the other kids' necks. Then, since everyone else was still busy with their talent show costumes, she went over to the computer and played games while the others glued, stitched, painted, and sprayed the different parts of their outfits. Everyone was content until Karen marched downstairs and said she needed to use the computer to write the treasurer's report for the High School Grounds Beautification Committee meeting tomorrow. When Lexie tried to argue with her, Karen raised one eyebrow and asked whether Lexie had gotten permission to "mutilate Mother's good black cape." At that point, Lexie and her friends exchanged glances and decided it was time to call it a day. The four of them packed up their costumes and trooped upstairs, leaving Karen behind efficiently entering neat, accurate columns of income and expenses.

At the back door, Lexie told the kids good-bye and said she'd see everyone at school the next day. When they were gone, she began sniffing around the kitchen to see what her parents were making for dinner. There was no one at the stove, but the aroma told the whole, revolting story. *Yuck!* They were having liver and onions. As she glared into an open pot, Daniel wandered into the kitchen. "Is that what I think it is in there, Lex?" he asked.

"I'm afraid so," Lexie said glumly.

Daniel's face took on a look of disgust. Then he turned around and practically sprinted out of the kitchen. Lexie knew exactly where he was going. He was making a beeline for the phone in the upstairs hall, where he would undoubtedly arrange to meet some of his jock friends so they could all go to McDonald's or Pizza Hut for dinner. It must be nice, Lexie thought, to be fifteen and a boy and free as a bird. When you were nine, you were forced to stay at home and eat whatever repulsive slop your parents put in front of you.

Depressed and sorry for herself, Lexie left the kitchen and walked into the living room, where she found Faith hunched over the desk, diligently doing her homework for the next day. Even while she slaved over her math problems, Faith produced a nonstop series of mournful sighs.

Lexie plopped down on the couch and took her latest library book from the magazine stand. It was called *Two-Thousand-and-Two Whacky Wriddles for Weirdos,* and Lexie was already up to number 602. It was the perfect kind of silly book to take her mind off things. Things like why her sister was such a crabby bore, or why Lexie was the only one of her friends who couldn't think of something original and interesting to do for the talent show.

By the time she'd reached riddle number 700, Lexie was smiling and giggling to herself as she read. When she read number 703, she laughed right out loud. "Hey, listen to this, Faith!" she chortled. "What happened to the librarian who fell into the copying machine?"

Faith didn't say anything, but she began irritatedly tapping the tip of her pencil on the desk top.

"Give up? She was beside herself! Get it? See, she fell in and made a copy of herself, so there were two of her, and—"

"I get it, you little lamebrain! And if you don't shut up, *you're* going to get it! If you had any ability at all to comprehend the complexity of the kinds of problems you have to do in seventh grade, you'd understand why I have to have peace and quiet in order to concentrate. Of course, given your current study habits, it's most unlikely that you'll be in the honors math program in junior high, but I'll tell you anyway that Mr. Rodman, the honors math teacher, is the most evil, most vicious man on the face of the earth, and if you make so much as one teensy, little mistake, he ridicules you for the whole rest of the period till you want to crawl under your desk and shrivel up and die. So that's why I have to do this homework absolutely perfectly. So would you please either close your mouth or get out of here?"

Lexie was working on a scathing remark about the

living room being a free country when her mother came into the room. "Now this is what I like to see," Mrs. Nielsen said with a fond smile. "My two little girls, both concentrating on their Sunday evening homework."

As unobtrusively as possible, Lexie closed her riddle book, turned it over, and wedged it behind the nearest sofa cushion. But she needn't have worried about her mother's seeing what she was reading. Mrs. Nielsen was staring at Faith, who had whirled around and jumped to her feet.

"Mom!" Faith announced. "You don't have to say another word! I've decided you're absolutely right. I will be more proud of myself if I stop erecting mental defense mechanisms to protect my psyche. I'm ready to take a risk! Tomorrow in homeroom I'm going to ask Justin Dupree to go to the Sadie Hawkins dance with me next Saturday night!"

Lexie's mouth dropped open in surprise, and even her mother looked taken aback. As Faith swept past them out of the room, Mrs. Nielsen's face was puzzled. "I just came in to say dinner was ready," she said. She turned toward Lexie. "Do you know what happened to make her change her mind like that?"

Lexie shrugged. "Don't ask me, Mom," she said. "These days I don't have the slightest idea why Faith does *anything* she does!" She turned around and tramped into the dining room to choke down a dinner of liver and onions.

Six

As usual during a troop meeting, Lexie found herself staring at Mrs. Noble, wondering how on earth the woman had ever become a scout leader. She was the exact opposite of what a leader was supposed to be like. She always wore a Twin Cities Bowling Champs T-shirt and a pair of lime-green polyester pants, and she often came to meetings with her hair in pincurls and a hairnet. She spoke in a low gravelly voice, and she usually had a cigarette hanging out of one corner of her mouth. Sometimes, when she thought the girls were too busy to notice, Lexie had seen her sneaking a glance at the copy of *Soap Opera Digest* she carried around in her purse.

Karen, who was *still* a Girl Scout at the age of seventeen, had visited one of Lexie's scout meetings once last year. She'd taken one horrified look at Mrs. Noble and immediately gone into a state of shock. Right after the meeting, Karen had rushed home and insisted that her parents have Lexie transferred to a troop with "proper leadership." But Lexie had pitched a fit and refused to hear of it. For one thing, all her friends were in this troop. But for another, Lexie really loved Mrs. Noble. She thought her troop leader was friendly and funny and great. She couldn't imagine being in a regular troop run by a jolly, enthusiastic leader—in short, a leader who would probably have a personality just like Karen's.

Today, however, for the first time Lexie was wondering if Karen might not have been right about finding a new troop. Today Mrs. Noble was acting like a real pain. After she'd asked for the treasurer's report (during which it was mentioned that Lexie was two weeks behind in her dues) and made the kids vote on whether to make plaster paperweights or coat-hanger tie racks for their fathers' Christmas presents, Mrs. Noble had started going around the room, asking each girl to describe what she'd be doing in the talent show next Saturday. Mrs. Noble's daughter, Rhonda, who was a quiet, pale, sickly looking girl, had just finished shyly explaining that she planned to wash, blow-dry, and style her little sister's hair right on stage. Lauren Lindskog, whose older sister Barb was one of Faith's former best friends, described how she was going to sketch quick charcoal portraits of some of the people in the audience. Then it was Brooke Stewart's turn.

"I plan to recite the 'to be or not to be' soliloquy," she announced importantly, "from the play *Hamlet,* by William Shakespeare. I can say the whole thing in under one minute."

Behind her tinted glasses, Mrs. Noble slowly closed her eyes as if she might be getting a headache, but she didn't say a word out loud. Lexie exchanged quick glances with Cheryl, Suzy, and Debby. They were all making disgusted faces and pretending to throw up on the floor. Brooke had joined Troop 1037 only a few short weeks ago, but she'd immediately made her presence felt. After the first meeting she'd attended, the other kids had all agreed she was obnoxious, conceited, and full of herself.

Lexie couldn't stand Brooke, and normally, she would have been right over there with her friends, making fake barfing sounds with the best of them. But today wasn't a normal day. Today, she was sick with worry, wondering what she'd tell Mrs. Noble about the talent show. It was one thing to pretend to the kids that her performance was some kind of mysterious secret, but Mrs. Noble was a whole other ball of wax.

Lexie looked over at Cheryl, Suzy, and Debby one more time and wished it could be yesterday afternoon again. It had been Lexie's favorite kind of day. They'd all had so much fun just hanging out, talking Ut, working on their costumes, and listening to music. She tilted herself back on her folding chair and replayed the scene in her mind. She saw an image of herself, sitting on the basement floor, laughing and stabbing stitches into her vampire cape.

All at once, as she daydreamed about yesterday, a sudden startling idea flashed into her mind. Could it possibly be the answer? she asked herself. Then she shook her head. No, no, no. It was a ridiculous, outrageous, stupid idea. And besides, it would never work because how . . .?

"I think Lexie's somewhere else today," Mrs. Noble was saying in her raspy voice. "Do you want to come back to earth, babe, and tell us what you've got up your sleeve for Saturday night?"

"Uh . . . huh?" Lexie sat forward with a jolt, and her chair slammed back down onto the floor, almost folding itself up with her inside it. Out of the corner of her eye, she saw Brooke Stewart suppress a superior smile.

"Saturday night?" Lexie repeated dumbly. "You mean the talent show?"

"That's the only place *I'm* going Saturday night," Mrs. Noble chuckled. "Will you be there to keep me company?"

"Uh . . . well, yes, I guess. . . ." She caught sight of Cheryl's sympathetic expression. "That is, sure I'll be there."

"And what will you be doing for the show? Will you need any help with props, music, a tape recorder, or whatever?"

Lexie swallowed. "Well, see . . . I have an idea, but I'm not sure about . . ." Her voice trailed off, and she felt her cheeks turning bright red. She avoided looking over at her friends' faces.

Mrs. Noble came to her rescue. She might be gruff, but she wasn't mean. "Okay, Lexie," she said. "Just let me know if you need any help or want to talk about the show, or whatever."

Lexie suffered through the rest of the meeting in miserable, embarrassed silence. She was so absorbed in her problems, she hardly knew what was going on. When Mrs. Noble called for a show of hands on challenging Boy Scout Troop 93 to a bowling match, Lexie voted both for and against the motion.

The instant the meeting was over, she jumped up, grabbed her backpack, and charged out the door before

66

her friends could catch her. She ran all the way up the Fiftieth Street hill to Fremont. When she got home, panting for breath, the house appeared to be completely empty. Well, that was something anyway, she thought. She wouldn't have to deal with a bunch of prying eyes and nosy questions.

She wrestled out of her backpack, hurled it onto the living room couch, and hurried up the stairs to her room. She yanked open the door and immediately saw Faith, planted in her usual position in front of the dressing table mirror.

Without missing a beat, Lexie started backing out of the room again. The last thing she wanted this afternoon was a session with one of her sister's bad moods. Today she had a bad mood of her own to feel miserable about!

But before she'd gone two steps in reverse, Faith swung around on her chair to face her. "Don't think I didn't see you, twerp," she laughed. "I have eyes in the back of my head."

Lexie's eyes grew wide. Could her ears be deceiving her? Had Faith really laughed? Could it be that her sister was actually *cheerful* today?

Yes, yes, it was true. Faith was getting up and almost dancing around the room! Then, wonder of wonders, she came over and gave Lexie's shoulders a little squeeze. Lexie thought she might faint from astonishment.

"The best thing happened today, twitface," Faith announced.

Lexie could think of only one thing that could possibly have made Faith this happy. "Justin Dupree got hit on the head and said he'd go to that dance thing with you?" she asked.

A cloud passed over Faith's face. "No, no, no, you little moron!" she said. "I didn't even ask him. See—"

"But you told Mom you would! I heard you myself. Yesterday in the living room you said—"

"Shut *up* and let me tell you what did happen! See, before I even saw Justin this morning, I ran into Becky Brady. And she told me that she and Shelly Perkins and Toni Jones have decided not to ask any boys to the Sadie Hawkins, so . . ."

"Shelly Perkins and Toni Jones?" Lexie interrupted. "Who *are* these kids anyway? What happened to Barb and Kathy and those other girls you hung out with in sixth grade?"

For a moment, Faith's face became puzzled. "I'm not really sure," she said slowly. "I mean, I see them around school and everything, and we always say hi, but we don't have the same lunch period or any of the same classes . . . and it just feels like we don't have that much in common anymore . . . or something." She frowned in thought and then suddenly seemed to recall what she'd been talking about before. "But what does that have to do with the point anyway?" she said in irritation. "The point is that Becky and Shelly and Toni are my friends *now,* and they're all going to the dance together as a big group, and they said I could go with them!"

Lexie shook her head doubtfully. "I don't know, Faith. After you made that big speech to Mom about taking risks and everything, I'm not sure she'll let you out of your commitment to your own self-worth and sense of honor."

"That's what you think! When I tell her how I've bonded with my female peers and formed a strong, sisterly support group, she'll be overjoyed to let me go with Becky and her friends."

"A strong sisterly support group," Lexie repeated in admiration. "I have to hand it to you, Faith. You're getting good at this stuff."

Faith grinned and patted her on the top of her head. Then she turned back toward the dressing table again. All at once, Lexie had an idea. If Faith was in such a good mood, maybe she'd be willing to hand out some helpful advice.

"Hey, Faith," she said. "Do you want to ride bikes around the lake? We could see if the food stand at the main beach is still open and get some of those giant Turkish Taffies, and . . ."

Faith was frowning at her reflection. "I'm giving up

candy this week," she said. "If I can lose four pounds by Saturday, I can wear my black leggings to the dance."

"Oh. Well, okay, we wouldn't have to eat anything. But I thought maybe while we were riding, I could talk to you about the talent show. See, I haven't figured out what I'm doing for it, but I do have this one sort of weird idea, and . . ."

She stopped talking when she noticed how Faith had thrown herself forward so she was practically lying down on top of the dressing table. "What are you doing, Faith?" she asked. "Trying to kiss the mirror?"

"I'm trying to see if the pores on my nose are clogged! But the light is so terrible in here, I can hardly see a thing. I wonder what Mom and Daddy would say if I asked for a makeup mirror for my birthday."

Lexie wondered what Mom and Daddy would say if she rushed across the room and ripped out a giant fistful of Faith's thick brown hair. "Have you been listening to a word I've been saying?" she asked indignantly.

Faith sat back down and started scrabbling through the drawer for her tweezers. "Uh . . . sure, I was listening, motormouth. You were talking about . . . uh . . . some kind of show . . . or . . . what was it again?"

"Oh, never mind," Lexie snapped. "I'll ride around the lake without you."

Riding bikes around Lake Harriet had always been

70

one of Lexie's favorite activities, but now, as she climbed on her bike and headed west toward the Forty-ninth Street hill, she couldn't really get excited about going. For one thing, going to a lake was a lot more fun in the summer, when you could jump into the water at the end of the ride. But also, Lexie realized, she never had much fun when she did things all by herself. It was just too boring when there was no one around to talk to or laugh with or even have a fight with.

She reached the top of the end of Fremont and turned left onto Forty-ninth Street. As she sped down the hill, her bike went faster and faster, and she remembered how she and Faith and their friends always used to automatically start racing whenever they came to this part of the road. Of course, Faith always won by a mile—and then gloated about it for the rest of the day. But today Lexie was feeling so lonely she would almost have liked the chance to listen to her sister brag.

After two more blocks, she reached Lake Harriet. She rode right up to the water's edge, where she bounced onto the rocky dirt path that circled the lake. She decided to go toward the right, in the direction of the main beach, so she could check out the food stand. After about fifteen minutes of steady pedaling, she reached her goal and broke into a grin. The food stand *was* still open.

She jumped off her bike, parked it next to the path, and headed toward the small, white building. As she went, she felt her mouth begin to water. She could already taste the sticky, chewy, banana-flavored taffy.

Then, as she was just about to reach the stand, she stopped short. What was she thinking of? She didn't have any money! Faith was the one who always brought money! Lexie always forgot hers—or else she didn't have any in the first place. There was no way she could buy any Turkish Taffy today.

Sadly, Lexie watched a little boy go up to the window and order the exact same kind of candy she wanted. With her hands in her pockets, she walked away from the food stand and wandered over to the deserted swimming beach. As she stood in the sand, staring out at the greenish gray water, she remembered the time she and Faith had caught a sunfish there, using only a plastic bucket and their bare hands. They'd taken the fish home, put it in an old fish tank, and named it Sunny. Of course, Sunny had died a few days later, and Faith had accused Lexie of forgetting to feed him, and they'd had a big fight about it. But it had still been fun catching him. An adventure. The kind of stuff sisters did together, Lexie thought. "Or *used* to do," she said out loud. "When I *had* a sister!"

She reached down and grabbed up a handful of small rocks. Last summer, she'd finally learned how to throw a rock so it would skip once on top of the water. Faith, her mother, her father, and even Karen could all make a rock skip two times, but Daniel held the Nielsen family record of seven skips. He acted as if it were no big deal, of course, but it seemed incredible to Lexie. Night after night, she lay awake in the dark, fantasizing about doing just one single thing as amazing as skipping a rock seven times. She felt that something like that would make her happy for the rest of her life. But to Daniel it was just a normal everyday thing!

In one way, Lexie knew she was jealous of all the things Daniel could do. But in another more secret way, she was really very proud of him and all his swimming trophies and soccer championships. Even though it really didn't have anything to do with her, she still felt as if she got to share a little of his glory, just because he was her brother. Of course she could never say anything like that out loud. Daniel was definitely not the kind of person you could spill your guts to.

As she thought about her brother, Lexie picked over the rocks in her hand, trying to choose the best one to skip. She ran her fingers over the smooth, flat surface and tried to remember how Daniel always did it, holding his arm straight out to the side and keeping the rock absolutely level. Then she placed the rock in her hand, drew her arm back, and threw.

The rock sailed out over the lake, whirling in circles as it went, but staying perfectly flat, just the way it was supposed to. At first, it looked like it might keep on going forever. But all at once, it dipped down once, just barely nicked the surface of the water, and popped up into the air again.

Lexie watched the rock making its second dip. She'd never had a rock skip more than once before, but this one was really going strong. "Yay!" she cheered from the shore, as the rock bounced back up into the air again. "Two skips!" Then her mouth dropped open. Was her rock actually going to keep on going after the *second* bounce?

Yes! It hit the surface of the water one more time, rose up, and then sank with a *plonk*. "Hurray!" Lexie screamed. "I did it! I skipped a rock three times! That's only four times less than Daniel. I'm second in the whole family!"

Right away, she knew she had to go home and tell everybody what had happened. If only Faith had come to the lake with her, she would have had a witness. Now probably no one would believe her. But she still had to tell them.

She ran back to her bike, climbed on, and started back the way she'd come. Twenty minutes later, when she neared the bottom of the Forty-ninth Street hill, she started pedaling furiously, determined to stay on her bike the whole way to the top. She got off to a good start. But, about three-quarters of the way up, her pace got so slow and wobbly, she had to get off. Still, she

74

told herself as she walked the rest of the way to the top, it wasn't bad. She'd been able to stay on her bike longer than she ever had before.

When she reached home, she jumped off her bike and let it fall over on its side on the lawn. She ran in the front door and almost crashed right into her mother, who was standing by the couch, reading a piece of paper.

"Hi, Mom," she said breathlessly. "Guess what just happened down at the lake?"

"What's this, honey?"

"I don't know what you're talking about, Mom. But anyway, just let me tell you—"

"I'm talking about this notice I found in your backpack."

Lexie was puzzled. What notice? She hadn't gotten any notices at school today. She tried to figure out where the paper could have come from, and then all at once, her heart flip-flopped and sank right down to her feet.

Oh no! she thought. Mrs. Noble! The troop leader had a habit of stuffing notices in the kids' backpacks before the end of the Scout meeting each week. Lexie had forgotten to look in hers. Her mother had found the notice. And now the whole family would know about the talent show.

Seven

"I'm surprised at Roberta Noble," Mrs. Nielsen said as she poured lo-cal dressing on her salad at dinner that night. "She's given the girls less than a week to get ready for this talent show. It really isn't enough time. She should have announced it sooner."

The spaghetti noodle Lexie was chewing suddenly tasted like a piece of dried-up string. "Ummm, Mom?" she said. "Don't you remember the show being . . . ummm . . . *mentioned* one night a few weeks ago?"

Mom frowned and poked at a cherry tomato with her

fork. "No, I don't remember, Lex," she said. "But I suppose my mind could have been on something else." She chewed for a moment, gazing at Lexie in thoughtful silence. "Have you been thinking about what you'd like to do for the show?" she asked.

"Well, um, sort of, I guess," Lexie mumbled. She glanced over her shoulder at the front door. Where the heck was Daniel tonight? she asked herself. Why couldn't he come barging in and drip sweat everywhere and distract everyone's attention the way he usually did?

Desperately, she turned toward Karen, who was busily twirling her spaghetti onto her fork. "Guess what, Karen," she said brightly. "I've been meaning to ask you something about the high school library. You know, we've been studying library skills in fourth grade for several weeks now, and I was wondering if you're using the same numbering system we're learning about."

Faith snorted, but Karen looked up from her plate in pleased astonishment. She beamed at Lexie and started to answer. But Mr. Nielsen, who hadn't really been listening to Lexie's question, suddenly interrupted. "I was in a talent show once," he said. "Or, more accurately, my dog and I were in one together. I'd trained him to do a whole series of complicated tricks, and believe you me, it was hard work for both of us. But it paid off because he really came through the night of the performance. Old King was the hit of the whole show."

"I think talent shows are a wonderful opportunity," Mrs. Nielsen said. "An excellent medium through which children can truly self-actualize."

"Isn't it time for the riddle game or something?" Lexie asked. She looked hopefully at her father, but he seemed to be absorbed in slathering butter onto a roll.

"Remember the time I was in a talent show?" Karen asked the group. "I had that portable chalkboard, and I demonstrated the dos and don'ts of researching material for a nonfiction report."

"I certainly do remember it," Mr. Nielsen said, taking a bite out of his roll. "Your third grade teacher wrote you a special letter commending you on all your hard work and careful planning."

Suddenly, something snapped inside of Lexie. She slapped her hand down hard on top of the table. Her fork popped up into the air and clattered onto the floor. "Well, don't expect to get any special letters about me!" Lexie screamed. "Because I'm not even planning to be in the show! And there's no reason for all of you to start nagging me to change my mind! I don't have any talents, and I don't belong in a talent show! And that's that!"

As a shocked silence filled the air, she pushed back

her chair and jumped to her feet. Then, with angry tears running down her face, she ran out of the dining room, narrowly missing crashing into Daniel, who had just tramped in through the front door. Without so much as a glance at her brother's surprised face, Lexie raced up the stairs to her bedroom.

Fifteen minutes later, a quiet knock sounded on the door. Lexie called out a shaky, "Come in," and braced herself for the upcoming rap session with her mother. To her surprise, her father came into the room. He was carrying her plate with the remains of her spaghetti on it.

"I know you always lick the plate when we have spaghetti," he said. "So I thought I'd bring it up here so you could slurp up the last few noodles."

Lexie sniffled, but she tried to smile at her father. She took the plate and picked up a noodle with her fingers. "Thanks, Daddy," she said. "You can go now."

"Not until you tell me why you're making a federal case out of this talent show business. And why you went screaming out of the room like that downstairs."

"What's the big deal about screaming out of the room?" Lexie asked, slurping up another noodle. "Faith does it practically every single night!"

Her father sighed and sat down on the bed. "Faith's going through kind of a hard time right now, kiddo."

"She's kind of a hard time all by herself!"

Mr. Nielsen smiled. "I guess I can't really argue with that. Sometimes I wonder if we'll all survive." He rubbed his chin and looked sideways at his daughter. "Don't try to distract me, Lexerino. I came up here to discuss *you*. Not Faith."

"Well, there's nothing to discuss. I don't want to be in the talent show, and that's that. But Mom's going to try to make me."

"No she isn't. We talked about it downstairs just now, and your mother and I agreed that if you feel that strongly about it, you shouldn't have to be in the talent show if you don't want to."

Lexie sat up straight and let out a whoop. "Really?" she cried. "That's just great. Good old Mom! You know sometimes I think I'm really not fair to her all the time. Maybe I could . . . oh, I don't know, help out more around the house, or something."

"You could start right in this room, kiddo. Your half looks like it's been raided by a band of Visigoths."

"Right! I will. First thing tomorrow, I'll clean it all up. And I'll keep it clean for the rest of my life." She got to her feet and carried her spaghetti plate toward the door. Then she turned around to stare suspiciously at her father, who was still sitting on the edge of her unmade bed. "Daddy," she said slowly. "Why are you still sitting there? I mean, we settled the problem about the talent show, right?"

"Right. We settled it. You don't have a single talent,

so you're not going to be in the show. And if you can be happy with that decision, we won't say anything more about it."

Lexie's heart started sinking again. Well, it figured. It had just been too simple. She should have known. Concerned parents like hers *never* let you escape that easily. "What do you mean 'if I can be happy with that decision,' Daddy?" she said. "I'm wildly, ecstatically happy with that decision!"

"Right," her father said again. "You're wildly, ecstatically happy that all your friends are going to be in the show . . ." He paused, and gave her a significant look. "I assume they're all going to be in it?" Lexie nodded dumbly, and Mr. Nielsen kept on talking. "You're wildly, ecstatically happy that all your friends are going to be in the show and that you are the only one of them who has no talent whatsoever?"

Lexie groaned. What was going on around here? Had her father been taking rap session lessons from her mother, or what? She put her plate down on the floor and came back to the bed to sit next to her father. "All right, Daddy," she sniffled. "I admit it. You've dragged it out of me. I'm *not* happy about that. How could I be? The other kids are all having fun making costumes and practicing and everything, and I don't have anything to do, and it makes me feel terrible. But what can I do about it, Daddy? I really don't have any talents!"

Mr. Nielsen shook his head. "Well, I just refuse to accept that, kiddo. Why, what about the piano? You play the piano, don't you?"

"No I don't, Daddy. Not anymore. Don't you remember? I hated my lessons so much, Mom finally let me quit. And besides, I never practiced, so I never learned anything anyway. Even Mrs. Larsen, the teacher, said it was hopeless."

"Well . . . all right, so you don't play the piano. But what about swimming? You're pretty good at that."

"Give me a break, Daddy! How am I supposed to swim across the stage in the basement of a church?"

"Ah yes, I see your point. Well, perhaps you could wear a suit and demonstrate the proper way to do the strokes."

Lexie stared at her father in horror. "You're kidding, right?" she asked.

Mr. Nielsen shook his head again and got to his feet. "All right, I give up, Lexie," he said, "I can't tell you what your talent should be anyway. You're the only one who can decide that." He moved toward the door and then turned around to face her again. "But I can tell you what a talent is—it's something you like to do . . . something you can do well . . . something you don't mind working hard on—spending time to improve. It might be something you take completely for granted, that you've never even thought of as a talent. You may not even know what all your talents are for a long time. But believe me, kiddo, you've got lots of them. You just have to put in some time and effort, and you'll figure out what they are." He started out the door again and then turned back one more time. "By the way," he said, "it's your night on dish crew, so blow your nose and hustle downstairs on the double."

As Lexie watched the door close behind her father's back, she heaved a long, gusty sigh that was worthy of Faith. Why did he have to come up here, anyway? she asked herself. She knew he'd just been trying to help, "to make her feel better about herself," as her mother would have put it. But he'd really made her feel worse than ever.

It was always worse when they were counting on her, somehow. Now she knew her parents were hoping she'd search her soul and uncover some great pile of hidden talents. But they didn't know Lexie as well as she knew herself. She *had* searched her soul for a talent again and again, and she'd always come up empty-handed!

Now there was no choice about it. She would have to get a stomachache the night of the talent show. It was really the only possible solution. It would be so painless. So simple. So easy. So why did it make her feel so miserable whenever she thought about doing it? She sighed again and lay down on her face. Then, in what was getting to be a regular habit, she started crying into her pillow. She cried so hard she forgot all about going downstairs to do the dishes.

Eight

The answer came to Lexie in school the next Friday afternoon, right in the middle of struggling to add one-third to one-quarter. She was halfheartedly scribbling on her paper, attempting to convert both fractions into sixths, when the idea flashed into her mind. It was more or less the same idea she'd thought of at the scout meeting on Monday. But this time, it was different. This time, the idea had changed into something that maybe, just *maybe,* could work.

Lexie concentrated so hard on seeing the image in

her mind that she pressed down on her pencil until it snapped. The point flew across the aisle and hit Stevie Crawford on the hand. Stevie looked up in surprise, but Lexie was still thinking so hard she didn't notice. Even when her teacher, Mr. Snyder, tapped her on the shoulder, she didn't come out of her fog. He asked her if she had the solution to the problem, and she said, "Yes, I think maybe I do!"

"Then why are you doodling a picture of Merlin the Magician in the answer space?" he said, pointing to her paper.

The whole class laughed, but Lexie didn't care. The instant Mr. Snyder turned his back again, she tore off the corner of her math paper and used it to write a note to Suzy. She passed it across the aisle and watched intently while it traveled from hand to hand to her friend's desk. When Suzy finally read the message and gave her the thumbs-up signal, Lexie grinned. After that, she hunched down over her math problems again. But she could barely see the numbers on the page. She was too excited about her new idea. And too worried about whether she'd really have the nerve to actually stand up in front of a crowd and *do* what she was thinking.

She was still excited and worried two hours later as she headed up Fiftieth Street toward her house. After school, she'd raced to the library for ten minutes and then hurried straight to Suzy's. She'd stayed at her friend's house just long enough to fill a garbage bag with materials from Mrs. Frankowski's sewing room. Now she was hurrying home with the bulging plastic bag under one arm and a fat pile of books under the other. She planned to get started on her project immediately, but even so, she'd barely have enough time to get ready. Why couldn't she have thought of the idea earlier in the week? she asked herself. Now she was going to have to work this afternoon and all day tomorrow in order to be prepared for the show tomorrow night.

Thinking about all she had to do made her walk faster, and she reached home in record time. As soon as she swept through the front door, she dashed toward the basement, not even bothering to stop in the kitchen for her usual handful of chocolate-covered granola bars. But downstairs, after she'd spread out all her supplies on the basement floor, she remembered a long-lost container of silver glitter left over from last Halloween. She thought it might be tucked away in the back corner of one of her dresser drawers upstairs. If she could find it, it would be perfect for what she needed. She raced back up both flights of stairs and yanked open her bedroom door.

She charged into the room and almost tripped over the pair of sandals she'd left in the middle of the floor the day before. Then she noticed something strange. Why was it so dark in the bedroom in the middle of the afternoon? Why were all the curtains pulled shut? And what was that horrible squawling noise? It sounded like Tiger, the cat from next door, yowling when she was losing a fight with the calico cat from down the street. Except that now, it sounded like Tiger was right here in the room. And like she had a bad case of the hiccups. And like she was in terrible pain.

Lexie took a few more steps forward and realized she wasn't alone. Someone else was already in the room, and it wasn't Tiger the cat. It was Faith. She was lying face down on her bed, clawing at her blankets, and sobbing as if her heart would break.

Lexie hesitated by the door. She was sure her sister hadn't heard her come in. How could Faith possibly have heard a thing, with all that noise she was making? It would be easy for Lexie to slip out of the room again and sneak back downstairs to the basement. She had a lot to do, and there probably wasn't anything really wrong with Faith anyway. She was always hysterical about something these days.

Lexie made up her mind to leave, but just as she turned to go, Faith shuddered and gave another gut-wrenching sob. Lexie stopped short and turned around again. She knew that if the tables were turned and *she* were the one weeping on the bed, Faith wouldn't just walk out on her. Besides, this sounded like serious agony. Maybe something really terrible had happened. She walked over to her sister's bed. "Faith?" she asked. "Are you okay?"

At the sound of Lexie's voice, her sister froze and choked on a violent hiccup. Then she grabbed her pillow with both hands and pulled it over her head.

"Go away!" she screamed in a muffled voice.

"But what's the matter? Did something happen?" Lexie was seized with a horrible thought. "Did something happen to Mom and Daddy . . . or Karen or Daniel?"

"No, you stupid little ignoramus! Now get out of here!"

"This is my room, too, Faith," Lexie retorted automatically. But then she stopped herself. How could she fight with a person who was too upset to even come out from under her pillow?

"I'll leave in a minute, Faith," she said. "Just as soon as you tell me what you're blubbering about. How bad could it be, anyway? Did evil Mr. Rodman give you an A-minus on your math homework, or something?"

All at once, Faith flung away the pillow and shot straight up in her bed. The way she sat up reminded Lexie of Count Dracula, rising up out of his coffin to grab a victim. But Faith's face didn't look anything like Dracula's. It wasn't pale and deathly. It was red and twisted and stained with tears.

88

"I'll t-t-tell you what's wrong if you'll leave me alone," Faith gasped out through her sobs. "And if you'll promise not to tell M-Mom. If I had to have a rap session right now, I'd . . . I'd . . . I'd smother myself with my own pillow!"

Lexie made heart-crossing signs on her chest. "I promise."

"It's . . . it's . . . B-B-B-Becky Brady!" Faith stammered on. "R-R-remember how I told you she said she and those other girls weren't asking any boys to the Sadie Hawkins dance, and they said I could go with them in a big group?"

Lexie nodded without speaking. Somehow she'd known all along that this had to do with the stupid dance.

"Well, anyway, today, I found out . . ." Faith stopped talking as a new flood of tears started out of her eyes. "I found out . . ." She took a long, shuddering breath and tried again. "I found out that Becky and Toni and Shelly all changed their minds. They *did* ask boys to the dance. And they weren't even going to bother to tell me!"

Lexie swallowed hard. Wow, she thought. Kids in middle school could really be mean! If her friends ever did anything like that to *her,* she'd feel like killing them. And herself, too! "Gosh, Faith," she began. "that's really—"

But her sister cut her off. "I'm not finished!" she said

hoarsely. "It gets even worse." She gulped for air and wiped her eyes with her fingers. "Guess who Becky— my dearest friend in that whole dumb school—guess which boy she asked to the dance?"

Lexie didn't have to guess. With a horrible certainty, she knew the answer instantly. "Becky asked Justin What's-his-name!" she gasped. "Even though she knew you *didn't* ask him because you thought you were going with her and her friends!"

Faith nodded and immediately began sobbing with new strength. She lay back down and flipped over onto her face. Once again, she grabbed her pillow and put it over her head. Lexie got up and tiptoed out of the room.

She spent the rest of the afternoon down in the basement, quietly working with her talent show materials and books. She was absorbed in what she was doing, and the costume was turning out exactly the way she'd wanted. Still, a lot of the fun had gone out of the project. Even while she was whirling around in her outfit in front of the basement bathroom mirror, she was thinking about Faith, crying upstairs in the bedroom. And she was wondering whether all her friends would turn into cruel, back-stabbing creeps when they started seventh grade.

The minute she heard her mother's car pulling into the garage, she hastily stuffed her costume into the old clothes trunk and ran to open the basement door. She intended to tell her family she'd changed her mind about being in the show, but she still didn't want them to find out what she was planning to do for it. Once they knew her idea, they'd immediately start asking a million questions about the whole thing, and that would just make her more nervous than ever.

"Hi, little Lexie!" her mother said when she saw her in the doorway. "Your timing couldn't be better. There are six bags of groceries in the trunk. If we each take three, we can make it up in one trip."

Good old Mom, Lexie thought as she staggered up the stairs with her load of bags. She can't look at a person without thinking of something worthwhile for her to do! She dumped the groceries on the kitchen table and tried to slip out of the room. But her mother was too quick for her.

"Now you can help unpack them, honey," she said. "And then you can set the table for dinner." She consulted a complicated chart on the front of the refrigerator. "And then please go find Faith. It's her night to help with dinner preparation. Karen's on dish crew."

And Daniel gets off free as a bird, as usual, Lexie said to herself. She wondered what kind of athletic practice her brother had this time. Out loud, she said, "Say, Mom, I think you'd better leave Faith alone tonight. She said she wasn't feeling good after school."

Her mother's face was immediately concerned. "Oh dear. Did she say what was wrong? I'd better go upstairs and check on her."

"No, Mom!" Lexie said quickly. "She said it was no big deal. She just wanted to lie still and rest. She's probably asleep now anyway."

Mrs. Nielsen frowned and looked as if she still wanted to go upstairs. Lexie thought fast. "And besides," she lied, "Faith and I switched dinner crew assignments for tonight, so it's my turn to help. What are we having anyway?"

"Poached filet of cod," her mother answered. "And brussels sprouts. You can unwrap the fish now if you want to. It's in that pink paper over there."

Gross! Lexie thought, as she slowly unpacked the slimy slabs of raw cod. She hated fish more than anything in the world. But her father loved it, and her mother insisted the family eat it at least once a week because it was so healthful. And she wouldn't even put bread crumbs on it and fry it in deep fat, which was just about the only way Lexie could stand to choke it down. No, her mother always insisted on poaching the stuff, so it retained its nutrients—and was all white and gooey and watery on the plates.

An hour and a half later, Lexie was still thinking about how disgusting the fish had been. She was standing at the kitchen sink, loading the dishwasher and feeling bitter. Even though it wasn't her night, she'd been forced into dish crew service because, the instant dinner was over, Karen had conveniently remembered that she had to go to an evening chorus practice right that very instant. She'd rushed out the door without so much as clearing her own plate, and, since Faith was still upstairs and Daniel hadn't even come home yet, Lexie'd been the only one left to help with the dishes. Now she was stuck in the kitchen, worrying about her talent show project, halfheartedly scraping fish remains into the disposal, and wondering how in the world Karen had ever made it past the tryouts for the chorus. Her father carried in a pile of dirty dishes from the dining room table.

"Last haul, kiddo," he said. He peered into the partially loaded dishwasher. "Say, are you remembering to rinse these dishes off? If you stick them in all full of food like that, the garbage washes off and overloads the whole drainage system."

Lexie sighed. Her family never thought she did anything right. She started yanking the dishes back out of the dishwasher and rinsing them under the hot water. "By the way, Daddy," she said over her shoulder, "I've changed my mind about tomorrow night. I'm going to be in the talent show after all. So if you and Mom want to come, it starts at seven."

There was such a long silence behind her that Lexie wondered if her father could have left the kitchen without her knowing it. She turned around to look and saw him, standing stock-still in the middle of the room, grinning like the Cheshire cat in *Alice in Wonderland*. He didn't say a word, but when he turned to leave the room, he was practically bouncing.

Chalk up a victory for the parents, she thought, turning back toward the sink. Her change of heart had really made her father's day. Lexie knew exactly what he was going to do next. He was going to run right to her mother and brag about how he'd conducted the most successful rap session in history.

Sure enough, two minutes later, as Lexie was scrubbing the countertops, Mrs. Nielsen came into the kitchen and kissed her on the top of her head. "Daddy and I are so pleased you changed your mind about the talent show, Lexie," she said. "Are we allowed to ask what you'll be doing?"

"Uh . . . well . . . no, as a matter of fact," Lexie replied, putting down the sponge. "I'd rather not talk about it."

Her mother squeezed her daughter's shoulders. "That's all right, sweetie, I know you need your private space. I'm just proud you've gotten a handle on this thing and dealt with it in such a positive way."

As Lexie's mother talked, Daniel came in through the kitchen door and went directly to the refrigerator and opened the door. "Hi there, Daniel," said Mrs. Nielsen. "I saved you a serving of dinner. Let me just go and get your plate off the table for you."

The instant Mrs. Nielsen left the kitchen, Daniel spoke in a loud whisper. "What exactly was dinner, Lex?" he asked.

Lexie pointed to a dirty plate full of white and green leftovers. "Poached filet of cod and brussels sprouts," she whispered back.

Without a moment's hesitation, her brother yanked open the freezer, grabbed a half-gallon carton of chocolate chip ice cream, and sprinted out into the hallway and on up the stairs to his room. Two seconds later, Mrs. Nielsen came back in from the dining room, carrying Daniel's plate. "Now where in the world did he go?" she asked.

Lexie rinsed a dish and considered squealing on her brother, but quickly decided against it. For the moment, Daniel had her complete sympathy. The fish and sprouts had been bad enough the first time around. They would be even worse reheated in the microwave! "Uh . . ." she told her mother, "he probably went upstairs to wash up or something."

"Oh well," said Mrs. Nielsen. "I'll stick this in the refrigerator for him then." She opened the cupboard and took out a box of Saran Wrap. "I'm just sorry Daniel and your sisters won't be able to come to your talent show, Lex," she went on. "I know they'd all be proud of you. But Karen has a study date with that boy, Ivan, from the library, and Daniel has a soccer game. And Faith will be busy going to the dance with her friends." She put away the fish, picked up the sponge, and started rescrubbing the counter Lexie had just scrubbed.

Lexie was so startled, she slammed the dishwasher shut, and the dishes inside rattled and clinked in their slots. Oh geez, she thought. Faith hadn't told Mom about the dance yet! That was probably the main reason the poor thing was hiding upstairs in the dark!

Without saying anything, Lexie dried her hands and crossed the room to the refrigerator. She opened the freezer and hauled out the remains of the Mississippi Mud ice cream cake they'd had for Mr. Nielsen's birthday dinner three weeks ago. She cut off a giant slab and slapped it onto a paper plate.

Her mother looked up from the gleaming countertop and noticed what Lexie was doing. "Lexie!" she exclaimed. "You had two big bowls of sliced peaches right after dinner."

"I'm still hungry," Lexie said shortly. Without waiting for another comment, she yanked a fork out of the silverware drawer and marched out of the kitchen.

Upstairs, she found the bedroom still completely shrouded in darkness. But Faith wasn't rolling around and crying anymore. She was lying absolutely rigid on her bed. The instant she heard the door open, she started breathing loudly and evenly, as if she were sound asleep.

"Cool it with the snoring, faker," Lexie said. "It's only me. I brought you some of Dad's birthday ice cream cake from Dessert Delite. It's pretty ancient, but it still looks okay." She started across the darkened room and crashed right into the battery powered walkie-talkie set she'd left in the middle of the floor three days ago. "Ouch!" she yelled, juggling the floppy paper plate as she hopped around. "This is dangerous! Can I turn on the light?"

"No!" came the answer from the bed. "Go away."

Lexie had an idea. Cautiously feeling her way with her toes, she inched her way across the room toward the corner. When she bumped into the wall, she used her free hand to paw around on the top of the bookshelf. Aha! She found what she was looking for. It was the fragile old porcelain moon-shaped nightlight their mother had turned on every single night when they were little girls. Lexie wasn't sure the old bulb would still work, but, when she clicked the switch, a gentle white glow filled the room.

She waited for Faith to complain about the light, but there was complete silence from the direction of the bed. Lexie went back across the room toward her sister. "I brought you some of Dad's Mississippi Mud cake," she said again. "Your favorite kind."

"Take it away. I'm sick. Get out of here."

Just then, a piece of paper crinkled under Lexie's foot. She reached down and picked up an empty candy bag. "Reese's Peanutbutter Cups," she read in the dim light. "You're kidding! This is the kind of bag they only sell at Halloween time, Faith. You're supposed to be able to feed twenty or thirty little kids out of this bag! Are you telling me you ate this whole thing? What a pig! No wonder you're sick!"

Faith groaned and pulled her pillow back over her head. Lexie put the ice cream cake on the dressing table and sat down on the edge of her sister's bed. Faith didn't say anything, but she did move her feet over to make more room.

For a few long minutes, neither one of them said anything. At last, Lexie cleared her throat. "Guess what happened to me down at the lake the other day. I threw a rock and it skipped three times! Isn't that great?"

Total silence from under the pillow. Lexie cleared her throat again and plunged ahead. "I've been thinking about all this stuff, Faith," she said. "About Becky Brady and those other girls."

She waited for Faith to answer, but her sister didn't do anything but sigh. "So anyway," Lexie went on, "what I decided was that those girls are total slimeballs. Especially Becky Brady."

A bitter laugh came from under the pillow. "Thanks a lot, little miss psychiatrist. But for your information, Becky Brady is the only friend I have in the whole seventh grade."

"Aha!" Lexie exclaimed, like a TV detective. She made a fist and pounded the bed as she spoke. "That is where you are wrong! That is exactly the point I'm trying to make! Becky Brady is *not* your friend! She is a total slimeball. How do I know? Easy! Because a friend would never act like she did!"

Faith lifted up one edge of the pillow to answer. "Oh, what do you know about it?" she said wearily. "You're only nine years old."

"I know that," Lexie answered. "I know I'm only nine. But even nine-year-olds know what friends are. And Becky and those kids *aren't* your friends! They're creeps. And I think you're *lucky* you won't be going to the dance with such a big bunch of losers! I think you should call up your *old* friends from last year and find out what they're doing tomorrow night!"

Faith didn't say anything, but after a long minute, she started quietly, miserably weeping again. To Lexie's surprise, all at once, she felt her *own* eyes filling up with tears. Abruptly, she got to her feet and went to the closet. She opened the door, kicked away the pile of shoes and clothes she'd thrown on the floor before the last clean-up inspection, and got down on her hands and knees. After a long, hot, fumbling search through the dark, she discovered what she was looking for.

Clutching her find, she got to her feet and went back

over to the bed. "Here, Faith," she whispered. "I brought you Bananny."

Faith didn't answer, so Lexie placed the worn yellow bear on the edge of the bed, right next to the pillow. She started out of the room and then turned back for one more look at her sister. Then she blinked. She wasn't positive, but, in the beam of light coming in from the hall, she thought she saw Faith's hand slowly creeping out from under the pillow and clutching one of Bananny's battered old fuzzy ears.

Oh well, Lexie thought. It wasn't much, but it was better than nothing. For the second time that day, she tiptoed quietly out into the hall and left her sister alone in the dark bedroom.

Nine

The next night, Lexie's father made her favorite dinner—tacos with all the trimmings. Out of habit, Lexie stuffed her taco shell with spicy meat and then smothered it with shredded cheese, black olives, chopped tomatoes, and sour cream. She took one crunchy, sloppy bite and quickly pushed away her plate. The food in her mouth tasted like a spoonful of sand, and it was all she could do to force it down her dry throat. There was no way she'd be able to eat any more dinner tonight.

She looked across the table at Faith, who was already putting away her third taco. Lexie shot a sideways glance at her mother, to see how she was reacting to this obvious violation of the pig-out rules, but Mrs. Nielsen was sprinkling shredded lettuce on her own taco, carefully pretending not to notice what Faith was doing. Her mother, her father, and Faith had had a long, low-voiced converstion up in the bedroom that morning. It had lasted for an eternity, and it was obvious that Faith had finally poured out the whole story of Becky Brady's betrayal. At one point, Lexie had gone upstairs to get a book. When she'd come to the door of her room, she'd stopped and eavesdropped for a few minutes.

"Daddy and I feel that it's important that you deal with Becky and her friends honestly, honey," Lexie had heard her mother saying. "I mean, we all realize that many people your age are going through a difficult adjustment period in their lives and often lose sight of what's important, but there's still no excuse for what those girls did. If you go to them and tell them how much they hurt your feelings, maybe they'll think twice before they act this way again. Maybe they'll even apologize."

Faith had mumbled something into her pillow, and then Mr. Nielsen had taken over. "Well, if they *don't* apologize, Faith, it says something about what kind of people they are, doesn't it? Maybe you don't want to cultivate them for friends. Maybe you want to try to seek out people with better values—like those other girls you used to have over here all the time. What were their names . . . Betty and Karla?"

"Barb and Kathy, Daddy," Faith had said. "But . . ."

Lexie had perked up her ears to hear Faith say she had nothing in common with her old friends, but just then Karen had come out of her room and discovered her in the hallway. "Lexie!" she'd said in an outraged tone. "I'm shocked that you would listen in on such a very private, personal conversation. Have you no moral values whatsoever?"

Lexie had rolled her eyes, stuck out her tongue, and gone back downstairs without her book. She never knew what else her parents and Faith had discussed, but Faith must have convinced them that her life was completely miserable. Ever since the talk, her mother and father had been treating her sister with so much quiet understanding and unspoken sympathy, the house was starting to remind Lexie of the inside of a church.

"Mom, is there any more sour cream in the kitchen?" Faith asked in the soft, mournful tone she'd been using all day.

Mrs. Nielsen glanced at the huge glob of sour cream already on Faith's plate and frowned. But she didn't say anything. Instead, she pushed back her chair and said she'd check in the refrigerator. Lexie blinked in surprise. Normally, if the kids wanted something from the kitchen, they were supposed to get it themselves. Lexie decided her mother must be feeling *really* guilty because she'd encouraged Faith to get excited about the dance and then the whole thing had ended in such a hysterical disaster.

When Mrs. Nielsen came back into the dining room with the sour cream container, Karen announced it was time for her to go meet Ivan, the boy she was studying with that night. "If we finish going over *King Lear* early," she said, "the two of us might drop in on Lexie's little show. But if we don't make it, remind Daddy to take lots of pictures."

Everyone but Lexie laughed out loud at this comment. There was never any need to remind her father to take pictures. The problem was to get him to *stop*. Lexie could still remember how embarrassed she'd been at her one and only piano recital when her father had crawled right up on the stage to get a close-up shot of her fingers on the keyboard. She only hoped he'd be able to control himself tonight.

Daniel was reaching for the last taco. "Say, Lex," he said. "What time's this show of yours, anyway?"

Lexie stared at her brother in surprise. Daniel almost never said anything at the table, particularly not to her. But now, not only was he speaking to her, he even seemed to be aware she was going to be in a show that night! This was bizarre behavior for Daniel. During most meals, he acted like his head was off in a soccer game in the clouds somewhere, dribbling in and out among a bunch of imaginary players, kicking goal after incredible goal. But here he was, asking a normal question and acting as if he'd actually been listening to the conversation!

"The show's at seven," she said, still gaping at him. "How come you want to know?"

"Cause my game doesn't start till eight, and I thought I might stop by. If you don't want your taco, can I have it?"

Without saying a word, Lexie pushed her plate across the table toward her brother. This was unbelievable, she told herself. Now Daniel, of all people, was coming to the show! She felt like she might be sick.

"That's just wonderful, Daniel!" Mrs. Nielsen, who had to be just as surprised as Lexie, was beaming with pleasure and enthusiasm. Then she turned toward Faith, lowered her voice, and immediately changed her smile into a gentle but concerned expression of encouragement. "You'll be coming with us, too, won't you, Faithie?"

Lexie waited for Faith to say she'd rather swallow rat poison than come to a juvenile, infantile Girl Scout talent show. "Oh, I guess I might as well come along,"

Faith sighed. "Heaven knows, I don't have anything *better* to do."

There was a moment's uncomfortable silence while everyone thought about just why it was that Faith didn't have anything better to do that night. Terrific, Lexie thought. Now even Faith is coming to the show. Faith, my sworn enemy, the meanest, most critical person in the world, who just happens to be in the worst mood of her life!

Mr. Nielsen cleared his throat and put on his most cheerful face. "I have a nickel in my back pocket," he said heartily, "for anyone who can guess the answer to the not one but *two* terrific riddles I heard today."

He waited until everyone stopped chewing and looked in his direction. "The first one sounds deceptively simple. Ahem. What kind of jacket would you wear on the sun?"

"Oh that one *is* simple, Frank. A blazer, of course!" Now it was time for everyone to swivel their heads and stare at Mrs. Nielsen. As far as anyone could remember, it was the first time in history that she'd ever paid the slightest attention to the riddle game. And now she'd come up with an answer, just like that!

"Way to go, Mom," Daniel said through a mouthful of taco.

Mr. Nielsen was still looking at his wife in amazement. Then he cleared his throat again. "All right, Bar-

106

bara," he said. "Perhaps you'll be more challenged by the second riddle. Here goes. Why was the sunken pirate ship shivering on the ocean floor?"

No one at the table could think of an answer. Lexie stared at her father and tried to concentrate. Pirates, she thought desperately. Buccaneers, treasure, booty, Long John Silver, eye patches, planks, matey, shiver me timbers, crow's nest, masts, maps, peg legs . . . Zilch! All at once, her mouth felt hot and sour. None of the words worked! She absolutely could not think of the answer!

Slowly, she pushed her chair back away from the table and started to get up. "Excuse me," she said. "I have to go upstairs and get something."

Her father's face looked hurt. "Don't you want to hear the answer, Lexie?" he asked in surprise. "It's a tough one, but I thought for sure you'd guess it. Don't tell me you're giving up so fast!"

Lexie went around the corner of the table without speaking. "Well, all right," her father said. "I'll tell you the answer, and you'll kick yourself. The pirate ship was shivering on the ocean floor because . . ." he paused dramatically, "because it was a *nervous* wreck!"

Everyone laughed, and Lexie faked a ghastly smile. "That's a good one, Daddy," she gasped as she ran out of the room. Ten minutes later, Daniel stumbled on her, hunched over the toilet in the upstairs bathroom.

"Hey, Lex," he said, bending down to stare at her face, "are you sick or something? Do you want me to go get Mom?"

"No!" Lexie moaned. "No, don't get her." She got up, flushed the toilet, and reached for the plastic drinking cup in the toothpaste stand. "And please don't tell anybody you found me in here. I'm not really sick. I'm just . . . I'm just . . ."

Daniel patted her on the back, and she choked on her water. "You're just uptight," he said. "I know exactly how you feel. I get like that all the time, right before a game. Don't worry about it, Lex. It goes right away before you have to get out there and really do your stuff."

He thumped her on the back again and tromped out of the bathroom. Lexie stared after him. For the second time that night, her brother had surprised her. She'd never seen Daniel act the slightest bit nervous in his entire life. He was always so good at all his sports, it was hard to believe he'd ever had anything to feel uptight about.

She sipped some more water and gazed at her reflection in the mirror. Oh no! she thought. She looked horrible—pale and sickly with big bags under her eyes. She never should have stayed up so late last night, reading all those books under her blanket with her flashlight. But she hadn't been able to sleep anyway, and besides, she'd been enjoying herself too much to stop.

Now she was paying the price. As she stared at her white face, she felt a new wave of sickness come over her. She lay down on the cool floor in front of the toilet and moaned. Then she got up on her hands and knees, crawled over to the door, and snapped the lock.

Who would have believed it? she asked herself as she flopped back down on the floor. Two weeks ago, she'd been planning to get sick on the night of the talent show. And now, here she was on the real night, locking herself in the bathroom so no one would find out she really, truly *was!*

Ten

Forty-five minutes later, Lexie was sitting on a folding chair at the edge of the stage in the Unitarian church basement, watching Debby Figenbaum play "Twist and Shout" on the piano. Her friend was really outdoing herself up there. Debby had seemed a little nervous when she first walked onto the stage, but after she'd bashed out a few chords on the piano, she'd loosened up. Now she was jumping and dancing and twisting while she hammered the keyboard and shouted out the lyrics. The shiny costume she'd made in Lexie's basement flashed and glittered under the lights, and the hair on the fluorescent purple wig she'd bought at Woolworth's flew out around her head, just like a real rock star's hair. The parents and brothers and sisters in the audience loved it so much they could hardly stay in their seats. They were laughing and pointing and clapping all the way through Debby's song. The more they carried on, the more nervous Lexie got. She had to go on next, and Debby was going to be a hard act to follow.

The audience had also loved Cheryl and Suzy's lipsynching performance at the beginning of the show. The two friends had been hysterically funny. Cheryl had stuffed a pillow under her dress so she'd look as fat as Mama Cass Elliot, and she'd put on a long flowing 1960s kind of dress. Suzy had worn boots and tight jeans and ironed her fuzzy hair so it would look long and straight like Michelle Philips'. When they'd started to lip-synch, they'd hammed it up like a couple of professional comedians, waving their toilet-paper-tube microphones and pretending to sing all the different parts in the song. Naturally, all the parents and brothers and sisters had screamed with laughter during the whole thing.

In fact, a lot of the parents didn't seem to be able to stop laughing that night. They'd thought Lauren Lindskog's sketch of Mrs. Noble in her bowling shirt was hysterically funny. And, even though it wasn't supposed to be funny, some of them had giggled while Rhonda

Noble was washing and styling her little sister's hair. And even more of them had laughed when Brooke Stewart recited Hamlet's soliloquy in less than one minute—which she actually managed to do, although she was babbling so fast, you could hardly understand a word she was saying.

Normally, Lexie would have laughed herself sick during Brooke's soliloquy, too. But she was already too sick with anxiety to laugh at anything. For the fifteenth time that evening, she swallowed and told herself to relax. The last thing she wanted was to make herself throw up again, just when she had to go out on the stage. She could still taste the Pepto-Bismol she'd gulped down before the family left the house. It had helped calm her stomach, but she wasn't sure how long the medicine would be effective. She only hoped Daniel had been right when he said the sickness went away right before you had to go out and do your stuff.

When she heard Debby going into her final set of "ahhh, ahhh, ahhhs" in front of the piano, Lexie swallowed again and got to her feet. Then everyone was clapping and cheering for Debby, and Mrs. Noble was walking out to the middle of the stage.

"Last but not least," the troop leader said, "our final *mysterious* performance tonight is by Lexie Nielsen!"

Suddenly, all the lights went out at once. Someone gasped, and then everything became very still. In pitch blackness, Lexie marched out to the center of the stage and stood with her back to the audience. Mrs. Noble aimed one small spotlight at Lexie and turned it on.

Someone in the audience said, "ohhh," and then Lexie heard one solitary person start to clap. She was almost positive it was her father, but she couldn't worry about him now. She spread her arms wide so that the silver glitter stars and moons she'd glued to the back of her mother's velvet coat would shine in the light. Then she whirled around to face the crowd.

"I am the Wizard of Riddles," she intoned dramatically. "Welcome to the riddle challenge."

Someone chuckled, and then there was complete, dead silence again. Lexie squinted and peered out at the darkened rows of seats. She wished Mrs. Noble hadn't pointed the spotlight right at her eyes like that. It might look good from up front, but Lexie felt like a blind bat looking out from a shadowy cave.

She licked her dry lips, tasted Pepto-Bismol, and kept on going. "The Riddle Wizard challenges you," she said, "to produce a riddle, *any* riddle, that she cannot answer." She folded her arms high in front of her chest. "The wizard awaits her first challenge."

Again, there was complete, total silence from the audience. Lexie stood without speaking for the longest minute she'd ever experienced. Nothing happened. A few folding chairs scraped on the floor, and the silence continued. Lexie didn't move, but inside her body, her heart started to thud in panicky, uneven beats. Say something, somebody please! she prayed. How could this be happening? She'd been worried about not being able to *answer* the riddles—not about nobody even *asking* any riddles! What was she supposed to do now?

She was looking sideways at the piano, wondering if she could still play the recital song she'd learned when she was seven, when a little five-year-old boy in the front row got to his feet. "I know a riddle," he squeaked.

Lexie couldn't see the little boy, but she thought he was Brooke Stewart's bratty little brother, Chase. He'd been a real pain in the neck at the Labor Day family cookout, but right now, Lexie felt like jumping off the stage and smothering him with kisses.

"What's green and red and goes forty miles an hour?" Chase asked.

"Louder in the back!" someone shouted.

Lexie looked out at the audience and tried to smile in wizardly fashion. "The riddle is this," she announced. "What is green and red and goes forty miles an hour?" As she spoke, her mind was whirling. Good, good, good, she thought. That was an easy one. She'd heard that riddle at least a million times. But what in the world was the answer?

As she stared down at Chase, his face suddenly turned

114

into a pale white blob that looked just like a cotton ball. Purple and green spots swam back and forth in front of her eyes. Lexie's mind was a complete blank.

She forced herself to speak. "The wizard knows the answer," she said solemnly. "She will get back to you in a few minutes."

Chase put his hands behind his ears, stuck out his tongue, and made a loud spitting noise that resounded throughout the entire church basement. Lexie felt her face turn bright red. Holy moley, she thought. This was a bigger disaster than she'd possibly imagined! She hadn't even been able to answer the first riddle. And it was one she already knew! Her brain just wasn't working. She was doomed! She had to get off that stage as fast as she could. But how?

Just then, another chair scraped in the audience. "I have a riddle for the wizard," a girl's voice said. "Why was the sunken pirate ship shivering on the ocean floor?"

Lexie blinked in surprise. "Because it was a nervous wreck," she said slowly. And then she added, "Just like the Riddle Wizard." Everyone in the audience shouted with sudden, appreciative laughter, and a few people even clapped. Hey! Lexie said to herself with a big grin. I know who asked that riddle. That was *Faith*'s voice. *My sister* asked me that riddle because she knew I'd get it!

She took a step forward and peered down at the rows of people. Sure enough, Faith was standing in front of her chair, looking intently up at the stage. When her eyes met Lexie's, she winked and made a quick circular, swirling motion with her right hand.

At first, Lexie didn't have the slightest idea what her sister was doing, but all at once, she picked up on the clue Faith was trying to give her. "The Riddle Wizard has something else to say," Lexie announced. "The answer to the spitting child's riddle: What is green and red and goes forty miles an hour is: a frog in a blender!"

The audience groaned and laughed, and then several more hands shot up. "Here's an oldie!" a grandfatherly voice shouted. "How do you make an elephant float?"

Lexie felt an instant of anxiety, but then she remembered she'd read that riddle in one of her library books, under her blanket late last night. "Put it in a glass of soda pop and add two scoops of ice cream!" she responded. "Next?"

"What's the best way to catch a squirrel?"

"Climb a tree and act like a nut! Next?"

"Which side of a leopard has the most spots?"

"The outside! Next?"

By the third riddle, Lexie felt her brain shift into high gear, and she knew she didn't need any more help from anyone. The show went on, and the brothers and sisters and parents and grandparents continued shouting up riddles from the audience. The Riddle Wizard continued shouting back the answers. Every now and then, someone asked a riddle Lexie hadn't heard before. When that happened, she would whirl around and turn her back to the crowd to give herself a few seconds to think. Some of the time, she figured out the right answer, but if she couldn't, she made up an answer of her own, or tried to think of something funny to say—and then everyone laughed anyway.

For instance, when Cheryl's big brother, Gordie, asked, "What's yellow and clicks?" Lexie knew right away it was one of those unfair riddles where she wouldn't be able to work out the answer based on a pun. But it didn't matter at all. In fact, the audience seemed to think her made-up answer, "a lemon with a pacemaker," was a lot funnier than the real answer, "a ballpoint banana!"

As she stood on the stage, answering the riddles, Lexie's mind started to feel just like the computer they used for research at school, processing her data and searching for key words in her memory. Like the computer, she knew she wouldn't be able to get the answer if she didn't have the information in her data bank. But she didn't care if she missed a few. She was having fun, and it was obvious the audience was enjoying the performance. Even Faith didn't appear to be completely miserable. At one point, after Lexie guessed the answer to a particularly difficult riddle about the kind of shoes boa constrictors wear (snakers), she snuck a glance down at her sister and got a pleasant surprise. While Faith wasn't stomping her feet and shouting, "Hurray!" the way their father was, she did appear to be *almost* on the verge of smiling. Given what Faith's mood had been before they'd come to the show, Lexie regarded that half-smile as the first major miracle in family history.

She looked away from her sister and called on another person. Lexie was having so much fun, she felt as if she could go on answering riddles for the rest of the night. But, right after she guessed what the boy octopus said to the girl octopus (I want to hold your hand, hand, hand, hand, hand, hand, hand, hand), she saw Mrs. Noble making throat slitting motions at her from behind the curtain, and she knew she had to stop. "Enough!" Lexie suddenly shouted out at the audience. "The Riddle Wizard grows weary."

A flashbulb flashed in her face, and she looked down and saw her father, practically sitting on Mrs. Noble's elderly mother's lap in the front row. Mr. Nielsen was clutching his camera and inching forward on his knees, coming closer and closer to the stage. Good old Daddy, she thought. He never gave up. She decided she'd better finish her act before her father was actually up on the stage next to her, taking pictures of her tonsils as she talked.

118

"The Riddle Wizard has one more thing to say," she said quickly. "I wish to challenge you, the audience, with this riddle: What happened to the girl who swallowed a can of varnish?"

Her father was getting closer, and Lexie didn't really expect anyone to try to answer anyway, so she went right on talking as fast as she could. "The wizard will tell you what happened to the girl who swallowed shellac!" she said. "Like the Riddle Wizard, she had a very lovely *finish!*"

On the word *finish,* she bent over, threw out her arms, and made a deep, dramatic bow. Mrs. Noble obediently switched off the spotlight, plunging the room into darkness again. There was one split second of silence, and then everyone started wildly cheering and applauding. Lexie even heard someone screaming, "Brava, brava! Encore, encore!" but it sounded so close to the stage, she was positive it was her father again. She wished he'd shut up, of course, but she was too happy to feel really embarrassed about him tonight.

The clapping continued, and Mrs. Noble turned all the lights back on. Lexie came out for a regular bow, and the clapping got louder. Her father was too busy snapping pictures to clap, but Lexie saw her mother applauding and cheering along with everyone else. Karen must have rushed through *King Lear,* because she was smiling and waving from the back wall, where she was standing next to a tall, geeky looking boy who had to be her friend Ivan. Daniel was still there, too, clapping and whistling, even though his soccer game was due to start in less than three minutes.

Finally, Lexie spotted Faith, sitting off on a bench on the far side of the room. She was clapping, too, but she was also giggling with another girl, whom Lexie recognized. It was Barb Lindskog, Faith's old friend from sixth grade, whose younger sister Lauren had done the charcoal sketches in the show. From the looks on the two girls' faces, Lexie could tell they were probably making fun of their little sisters' babyish performances, but Lexie didn't even feel angry about that. She'd always really liked Barb, and she hoped Faith was discovering that the two of them had *something* in common after all. And anyway, nothing Faith did or said could make Lexie feel angry tonight.

Mrs. Noble led all the other girls out on stage for a final bow, and then Brooke handed the troop leader an enormous bouquet of roses. Lexie shot a sideways look at Cheryl, who was standing next to her, and they both grinned. "Typical Brooke," Cheryl muttered under her breath. "Kissing up to the troop leader."

"Well, she struck out this time," Lexie muttered back. "Mrs. Noble is allergic to flowers. She would have liked a new bowling shirt much better!"

They giggled and then followed the other girls back off the stage. Mrs. Noble was waiting at the bottom of

120

the stage stairs, sneezing into her flowers, congratulating everyone, and telling them how great they'd been. When she saw Lexie, she shook her hand and said, "You had me going for a minute tonight, babe. I thought I was going to have to come out on stage and pick you up off the floor! But you pulled it off. Pretty gutsy performance. How the heck did you ever learn all those riddles?"

Lexie knew she'd never be able to explain, so she just shrugged and grinned. She turned around to hug and congratulate Cheryl and Suzy and Debby. Then her parents rushed up and kissed and squeezed her as if she'd just performed at Carnegie Hall.

"Leave it to Lexie to steal the whole show!" her father boomed to anyone who'd listen. "You know, I taught her everything she knows."

"Hush, Frank, you're embarrassing Lexie in front of her peer group," her mother said. "Let's all go out for ice cream to celebrate. I'm starving."

"So am I!" Lexie said.

"Me, too," a voice said in her ear.

Lexie turned around and saw Faith standing right behind her. For a few seconds, she just stood there, looking at her older sister. Then Lexie cleared her throat. "Uh . . . gee, thanks, Faith," she mumbled. "For . . . you know . . ."

"Oh well," her sister interrupted impatiently, "it

wasn't really all that much. But when you choked on an easy riddle like that frog-in-the-blender thing . . . well, I had to do *something*, for gosh sakes!" She turned away from Lexie and tugged on her father's sleeve. "Let's go, Daddy!" she whined. "This isn't a hotel, you know. We're not supposed to spend the night here! Besides, I'm starving!"

Automatically, Lexie started to say, "Why don't you tell us something we don't already know?" But she stopped herself before any words came out. In thoughtful silence, she followed her parents out the exit to the parking lot, where they all climbed into their battered old Ford station wagon.

No, she thought, as she buckled herself into the back seat. No. Even though Faith was already back to being her mean old self again, Lexie wasn't going to start a fight with her tonight. Tonight was too terrific a night for fighting. Everything had gone too well. First of all, Lexie had had a fantastic time at the show. But more importantly, she'd discovered she actually did have one real, if slightly weird, talent. Who knew? If she thought a little harder, she might discover she had even more!

She shot a sideways look at Faith, who was sighing again and staring out the window, and all at once, she realized she'd made another important discovery tonight. She would have had trouble explaining it out loud, of course, but she knew the discovery was about

122

her and Faith and how things could change—but then not change, all at the same time. It had to do with being sisters and part of a family. And, for the moment anyway, it was making Lexie feel a lot happier than she had in a long time.

In the darkness of the back of the station wagon, she smiled to herself and rested her cheek against the cool vinyl seat cover. Then, as she dreamed about the enormous hot fudge peanut sundae she was about to order from Dessert Delite, her father started the car and drove off into the night.